She'd call his bluff.

Not for anything did she want Chase to know how much his offhand proposal had tormented—and maybe tantalised—her. It was a joke; it couldn't be anything else. If she said yes, he'd either have to put up or shut up, and she was certain he'd choose to shut up.

Suddenly *very* certain of that, Fay came to a halt at the edge of the patio and turned to him. "All right. Let's do it."

His gaze zoomed up to fasten on hers. "Then your answer is yes?" His gaze probed hers for several seconds.

Fay shrugged. "Sure. Why not?

This whole marriage idea was beginning to hurt. There'd been a time when she would have loved to have Chase Rafferty ask her to marry him, but he'd made a joke of asking her. Even worse, he'd made her *think* about marrying him, over and over and obsessively. And of course her dying heart had grabbed onto the idea like a lifeline.

Absorbing and powerful, Susan Fox is a compelling storyteller who explores the most heart-felt of emotions—her stories will have you reaching for the hankies!

Praise for Susan Fox:

'Susan Fox has an easy writing style that makes for fast reading. So fast, that when it is done you wish the story wasn't over.'
www.thebestreviews.com

In HIS HIRED BRIDE 'Susan Fox takes a classic plot and makes it her own by creating original, memorable characters and fresh, funny dialogue.'
—Romantic Times BOOKreviews

'When it comes to creating soft, vulnerable heroines and strong alpha heroes, Ms Fox has perfected the technique down to a fine art…'
www.thebestreviews.com

THE BRIDAL CONTRACT

BY

SUSAN FOX

DID YOU PURCHASE THIS BOOK WITHOUT A COVER?

If you did, you should be aware it is **stolen property** as it was reported *unsold and destroyed* by a retailer. Neither the author nor the publisher has received any payment for this book.

All the characters in this book have no existence outside the imagination of the author, and have no relation whatsoever to anyone bearing the same name or names. They are not even distantly inspired by any individual known or unknown to the author, and all the incidents are pure invention.

All Rights Reserved including the right of reproduction in whole or in part in any form. This edition is published by arrangement with Harlequin Enterprises II BV/S.à.r.l. The text of this publication or any part thereof may not be reproduced or transmitted in any form or by any means, electronic or mechanical, including photocopying, recording, storage in an information retrieval system, or otherwise, without the written permission of the publisher.

This book is sold subject to the condition that it shall not, by way of trade or otherwise, be lent, resold, hired out or otherwise circulated without the prior consent of the publisher in any form of binding or cover other than that in which it is published and without a similar condition including this condition being imposed on the subsequent purchaser.

® and TM are trademarks owned and used by the trademark owner and/or its licensee. Trademarks marked with ® are registered with the United Kingdom Patent Office and/or the Office for Harmonisation in the Internal Market and in other countries.

First published in Great Britain 2007
Harlequin Mills & Boon Limited,
Eton House, 18-24 Paradise Road, Richmond, Surrey TW9 1SR

© Susan Fox 2007

ISBN-13: 978 0 263 85455 8

Set in Times Roman 13¾ on 16¾ pt
02-0907-37871

Printed and bound in Spain
by Litografia Rosés, S.A., Barcelona

Susan Fox figures she's lived enough of her life in the city to consider moving back to the country. Her country dream home would include a few pygmy goats to take care of the lawn, a couple of ponies for granddaughters Arissa and Emma, a horse or two for herself, and whatever stray cats or dogs might happen by looking for a home. Until then, she fears she'll have to make do with a lawn mower, three always-up-to-something cats and two very naughty but adorable stray kittens. Susan loves to hear from her fans. You can contact her via her website at www.susanfox.org

CHAPTER ONE

THE late afternoon Texas heat was even more intense than it had been earlier, making the minor fence repair a feat of endurance rather than the mindless drudgery it usually was. Fay Sheridan felt another rivulet of perspiration streak down her cheek to bead on her jaw as she set the prongs of the last staple against a fence post. The bead of sweat fell as she hammered the staple into the wood, securing the loose strand of barbed wire. A few of the older wood posts along this stretch of fence needed to be replaced with T-posts when she got time.

Time. She felt the stifling weight of it as she pulled off her Stetson to blot her forehead and jaw on the sleeve of her plaid work shirt. She was overloaded with time these days. Months, weeks, days, hours, minutes…

There weren't many true seconds anymore. It was as if they'd all stretched to the length of minutes, and she was living some kind of slow-motion life, where the more she found to do, the more leftover time she was stuck with. She'd somehow lost her grip on the kind of days when hard, continuous work made time fly.

Fay put her Stetson back on and walked to her horse. The sorrel gelding had been dozing in the heat but he perked up when she put the hammer and bag of staples in the saddlebag, as if he hoped the workday was done. Thunder rumbled, and Fay glanced toward the western sky.

The thunderhead that had been building in the distance looked to be at least seventy thousand feet high, with others piling high on either side behind it. The massive, anvil topped cloud formations had blocked the sun, though the air was still hot and muggy and the sky overhead and behind her to the east was blue. The storm would be a big one, bringing an evening of hail and much needed rain, with maybe a tornado or two.

Fay mounted her horse and continued along the fence, scanning the four-strand barbed wire that separated her ranch from the much larger R/K Ranch. If the storm held off, she might be able to finish checking this stretch. She'd become almost fanatical about maintaining the miles of fence on her ranch, but then, she'd become fanatical about a lot of things this past year.

Constant vigilance and almost continuous hard work had helped her stay sane, providing her with purpose and restoring at least some sense of order. Life had become predictable again; at least she'd been able to create the illusion that it was. And yet the energy that illusion of predictability required had also leached what little vitality and pleasure life might still hold for her.

Which was probably why the oncoming storms brought an inkling of relief despite the frustration of having to leave a chore unfinished. The sameness of the past year had worn her down, but storms the size of this one banished a bit of that sameness. A long, much louder rumble of thunder sounded, and she drew her horse to a halt at the crest of a rise.

The massive clouds had churned closer in the few minutes she'd been riding, and parts of them were dragging rain shafts. She could tell when the wind picked up at ground level in the distance, and watched as it brushed down the dry grass like a giant, invisible arm sweeping across the land.

The sorrel warily turned toward the fence and pricked his ears forward expectantly, his nostrils flaring to catch the scent of rain as the first cooling wind gust reached them. The air temperature dropped several degrees, and Fay felt a light chill over her sweat-damp clothes. The first gust was quickly followed by harder, much cooler gusts, and the air filled with the scent of rain.

It didn't bother her that she was astride a horse on top of a ripple of land, not only high profile in open country next to a wire fence, but also carrying enough metal in her saddlebag to attract a bolt of lightning. Lightning could strike from miles away, but she felt no fear at the notion, and wondered fleetingly if she'd ever feel fear again. She'd already faced one of the most excruciating pains life could hold. After that, every other calamity paled in comparison, even the idea of being struck by lightning.

The sorrel began to fidget, but Fay tightened the reins to check his movement, more than a little mesmerized by the storm. Something about it mirrored the deepest places in her heart, places where despair warred against the will to survive, and her soul grappled with incomprehensible tragedy.

The black clouds of the storm roiled faster now, blotting out the western sky from north to south and rapidly filling the air above her. The rumble of thunder varied from muted rambling to crackling cascades of sound that tumbled from screeching highs to throbbing lows that trailed on and on.

She ought to turn the sorrel and ride to the house, but she couldn't seem to make herself start. Sheet-lightning whitened a cloud here and there, and occasional cloud-to-ground lightning pierced down to dance across the land.

Tendrils of spectral clouds dangled eerily nearby, but there was no sign yet of a wall cloud that signaled a potential tornado. Fat, intermittent drops of rain began to splatter the dry grass near the fence, kicking up tiny dust explosions here and there as the drops hit dirt.

The sorrel began to fidget again, momentarily distracting her. The horse was impatient for the shelter and safety of the stable. No doubt he wanted to outrun the storm and was confused about the delay. Any horse would be looking forward to the end of a workday, eager for a stall and a rubdown before a fresh pail of water and a measure of grain. The storm would make that idea even more attractive.

Fay had no similar eagerness for home and rest, and hadn't for a long time. The hardest part of the day, other than facing the start of a new one before dawn, was the time she had to finally walk into the big house, where the only person there was a housekeeper. Yet more often than not, Margie's work would be done and she'd have gone home.

Fay continued to watch the clouds, letting the growing danger send a tingle of peril through her to offset the bleakness she felt at the idea of going home to an empty house. The wind blew harder now, and the fat raindrops gave way to smaller, faster drops. The sky continued to rumble and flash, as if to warn her, and the anger she'd been numb to for months began to stir. Suddenly it burst into outrage.

The boys hadn't been given a warning; they'd never had a chance. One moment they'd been having the time of their lives learning to water ski; the next, they'd been struck by a boat and drowned. They'd barely had a hint of what was coming, and no chance to escape it.

The agony of that knowledge was unbearable, and her failure to come to terms with it this past year stoked the conflagration of pain and anger until she was wild with it. *If death meant to reach out for her now, too, then it could damn well get on with it while she was watching.*

The defiant thought was buttressed by an avalanche of self-pity. What did she really have left anyway, but a life of work and responsibility that was dominated by grief and loss and regret? Her heart had been crushed and sometimes she felt so hollow and hurt so much that she wasn't sure she could scrape up enough courage to face another moment.

One stroke of lightning could put a quick end to the relentless march of endless gray days, and the idea grew more tantalizing by the second. After weeks and months of being numb, the mounting chaos of dark feelings was overwhelming. The knowledge that she wanted to die made her feel even more defiant.

The sorrel began to prance again and toss his head, but Fay kept the reins tight, all but daring death to strike her down as brutally as it had her brothers. As if the storm was eager to accommodate her, the wind began to blow even harder. Marble-size bits of hail beat down with the rain, then abruptly stopped, and the sorrel tossed his head again, snorting impatiently.

Fay was so caught up in the storm and the anger that boiled impotently inside her that she was slow to distinguish the distant shouts over the roar of the wind. Once they caught her attention, the shouts became louder and more distinct.

Fay!

Run, Fay!

Go now—please!

The sound of her name in the roar and the urgent message jolted her.

Fay—don't do it!

Run!

Recognition struck her heart like a closed fist, and sent a rash of goose bumps over her skin. The world tipped, and she felt the fleeting touch of something other-worldly, yet familiar. Shaken to her soul, she glanced wildly around.

"Ty? Troy?"

She hadn't mistaken her brothers' voices, and yet she couldn't possibly have heard them call to her. As she continued to glance around and strained to hear their voices in the howl of the storm, she realized she was trembling.

The sorrel had taken advantage of her distraction and was moving away from the fence, though Fay's grip had frozen on the reins and she was still holding him back.

Her brain was in shock, and her heart all but bled with longing to hear those beloved voices again.

Had she lost her mind? The question burst into her consciousness, bringing a new torment. Her heart was pounding hard enough to make her chest ache as her thoughts ran crazily for an explanation. She knew her brothers' voices and always would, but to hear them so clearly, and to feel that otherworldly touch…

Fay loosened the sorrel's reins, still straining to hear their voices, but suddenly a little afraid she would. Maybe going crazy and hearing voices was the next turn in the downward spiral she'd been on, and the idea shook her up even more.

She couldn't deal with this, couldn't cope. The knowledge that she'd reached her emotional limit sent anxiety pumping through her. She urged the sorrel into a trot away from the fence in the rain-slick grass in an instinctive need to flee what she couldn't understand, but just as she signaled him into a gallop, the air suddenly went blindingly white. The simultaneous boom of thunder sent the sorrel shying hard to the side, taking Fay so by surprise that she lost her balance and clung to the side of the saddle.

A second flash and boom, even more blinding and deafening than the first, made the sorrel lunge the other way, literally pitching her from one side of the saddle to the other. At the same instant, his back hooves slipped and his backside started to go down. Fay managed to yank her left boot from the stirrup to keep from getting a foot trapped, but the sorrel caught himself and lurched awkwardly to his feet.

He barely got all four hooves solidly beneath him before he rocketed away, breaking her hold, and the hard, wet ground leaped up to slam the breath out of her.

* * *

Fay Sheridan had been different when her brothers were alive. Energetic, full of fun, her never-met-a-stranger personality had made her a stand out. Her younger twin brothers, Ty and Troy, had been a lot like her. Handsome, competitive, but in their cases, always up to something. Fay had handled them good-naturedly, tough and strict when they'd needed it, but managing to walk that precarious line between proud big sister and parent after their momma and daddy had died five years back.

Then a year ago, the world had tragically changed for Fay, robbing her of her brothers, but also stealing away the happy, vital young woman that nearly every single male in that part of Texas had taken note of. She'd become something of a hermit after those first weeks, exiling herself from the ranch community in general, old friends in particular, and neighbors when she could.

For the past year few people, other than her housekeeper and ranch hands, got more than a fleeting glimpse of her.

Chase Rafferty had been one of the few, regularly pushing his way into her life and into her business. That's why he was driving to the boundary fence late that afternoon. One of his men had seen Fay out this way, and since the weather service had issued multiple storm watches and warnings, Chase had decided to see if she was still out here. He didn't trust that she'd ridden on home.

The moment he'd seen the slim female atop the sorrel, he'd known he was right to investigate. The storm was almost on top of her, but instead of sensibly making tracks to shelter Fay was watching the clouds, frittering away precious minutes that could have ensured she safely reached home. It was foolish to gawk at a storm while she was so exposed to the danger of lightning, and in the case of this storm, it was suicidal.

And that's the real reason he was here. Fay Sheridan had lost her way and, despite the stubborn front she put up, he'd sensed the recklessness in her. Now he was seeing it, and he shoved down on the truck's accelerator to intervene as the big raindrops on his windshield changed to a wind-lashed deluge.

A bright flash of lightning and cannon shot of thunder was quickly followed by a second flash that struck close. The almost instantaneous explosion of thunder set the sorrel off and Chase watched through the rain-sheeted windshield as the horse started to go down, scrambled for footing, then bolted away without his rider.

The gate between Rafferty/Keenan and Sheridan land was more than a mile away, so he steered his big truck toward the fence. The impact of the truck against four strands of taut wire was minimal, but he felt a moment of resistance before the wire gave way. Once the truck was clear of the wire, he cranked the wheel to the left and circled to find where Fay had landed.

Now that he was facing the storm, the wind-driven rain made it all but impossible to see through the windshield. Wary of running her over, Chase levered the door open a little and leaned out in time to see Fay rise to her hands and knees.

The little idiot was alive.

Fay managed to stay conscious but couldn't breathe. She instinctively rolled to her side then to her stomach to pull in enough air to relieve the pressure in her chest. Her head was spinning and she was nauseous, but she made it to her hands and knees and panted while she waited for more strength. Her clothes were soaked, her shoulder, hip and knee were throbbing, and she had the headache of her life. She tried to get up, but couldn't do it yet, so she settled for moving a hand around until her fingers came in contact with the brim of her Stetson and dragged it close.

She thought she heard a pickup engine over the sound of the storm, but her ears were ringing so she wasn't sure. Anxiety went through her at the idea that she was still hearing things that weren't there, and the chill the thought left in its wake made her tremble. She didn't hear the heavy tread of man-size boots until just before someone caught her around the waist and lifted her to her feet.

Fay cried out against the pain and surprise of the sudden move, helpless to do anything but bite her lip to stifle another embarrassing cry as she was all but dragged to the open door of a white pickup. At least this was real, and her anxiety eased. Her rescuer gathered her up and lifted her to the driver's seat so suddenly that she had to close her eyes against the dizziness. She tried to move across the bench seat under her own power, but a pair of strong hands shifted her out of the way as easily as if she was a child.

Her rescuer climbed in after her, his big body bumping solidly against her bruised side, but Fay was too rattled and disoriented to move even an inch away from it. Besides, the heat of the shoulder to knee contact felt good, though the warmth set off another wave of the icy shivers that racked her.

A volley of hail hit the pickup roof, and the truck door banged shut. The engine revved as the pickup lurched backward, swinging around and nearly pitching her off the seat. The driver's hard arm kept her from falling.

Fay reflexively reached for it, but the

arm jerked down to shift gears as the pickup abruptly stopped then shot forward into a bumpy, fishtailing ride. Her nausea came back in direct proportion and she grabbed urgently for the driver's arm.

"Slow down!" she panted, too weak to do more than hang on to him with her good right hand. She was so dizzy she had to close her eyes again.

The low voice that shot back was blunt and offensively descriptive.

"We gotta funnel cloud about to blow up the tailpipe."

Fay felt a fresh surge of nausea as she recognized the voice. She made herself let go of his arm as he went on.

"Not that *you'd* care if a tornado dropped down on your head, but some of us would rather die of old age."

The sarcasm cleared her brain and she managed to focus briefly on Chase Rafferty's grim profile before she faced forward, her insides twisting with shame. And resentment.

Rafferty. Chase Rafferty, the biggest bull in the pasture, who regularly charged in where she didn't want him to be. Good fences and closed doors meant nothing to him. In all these months he'd been the one person she hadn't been able to keep away, the one person who hadn't allowed her to come to grips with the loss of her brothers in solitude.

Everyone else had gotten the message that she needed time alone and didn't feel like seeing anyone she didn't have to, but Chase always found a reason to butt in. The worst had been during those first weeks after the double funeral, when he'd come over at 7:00 a.m. four mornings in a row, pounding on her bedroom door to inform her that it was a workday and she had men standing around waiting for her say-so.

And of course he'd hung around in her

kitchen long enough to see her after she'd got dressed and come down for a quick breakfast. He'd been able to tell she had a hangover, but he'd waited until she'd finished eating to lecture her about the dangers of crawling into a bottle to numb her grief.

On the third morning, she'd come down to the kitchen after another loud awakening and threatened to do him bodily harm if he said anything more to her than "Good morning." That was the last hangover she'd had though, because she'd stopped drinking herself to sleep. When he'd come by at 7:00 a.m. on the fourth morning, she'd already gone out, working away from the headquarters so she wouldn't have to see him.

A few weeks later, he'd taken to phoning at the noon meal, wanting to know if she was going to show up for a cattlemen's meeting that night or if she had plans to go to some local event or social gathering that weekend. His message was clear: Get back to living. Her message to him, after she got a caller ID and stopped answering his calls or returning them, was: Leave me alone.

After that, he'd gone back to stopping by from time to time, only he'd started asking if she had thoughts about selling out. Short of that, he was looking for land to lease, and since she'd sold off part of her herd, would she want to work out a deal to let him run some of his cattle on her range?

Those were the times that had annoyed her the most. As if she was some wimpy female who'd never be able to hang on to her heritage by herself. His offer had stung her pride at the time, but later that sting had begun to undermine her confidence and make her feel like a failure. After all, Rafferty/Keenan was a huge operation, and the man who ran it had a knack for spotting problems.

And the fact that it had been Rafferty who'd seen her get thrown off her horse just now, Rafferty who'd picked her up and stuffed her into his truck, and Rafferty who was racing across the range to outrun a dangerous storm, was bitter comeuppance for her foolishness with the lightning.

Even more bitter was the idea that he'd seen her moments of self-destructive daring before her fall, and would no doubt soon let her know he had. That's why she'd started to hate the sight of him, and heartily wished she could target his Achilles' heel as mercilessly as he had hers this past year. She hated even more that men like him didn't seem to have any.

It was hard to remember now that there'd been a time—years actually—when she'd had a huge crush on Chase Rafferty. Even the idea that she might see him somewhere had given her a thrill. She would have loved to have his attention back then, though he'd seemed to be only marginally aware of her.

He'd had too many girlfriends, and she'd been a neighbor kid seven years younger, and far too inexperienced for an earthy man of the world like him. She'd worried for years that he'd marry one of his glamorous girlfriends, and when he hadn't, her hope that he'd finally notice her and ask her out had become acute.

Then the boys had been killed and she'd lost interest in Chase along with everything else. Though he was still as ruggedly handsome as ever and remained the most sought after bachelor in their part of Texas, Fay was immune to him now.

And she was still nauseous from the rough ride. The longer the trip went, the more aches and pains made themselves felt, but she'd bite her tongue off before she'd complain. She couldn't let herself get sick, either; that would be the ultimate shame if it happened with Rafferty around. Surely they'd reach the main house at her place soon.

They finally drove out of the rain and were now ahead of it. Chase turned onto one of the better pasture roads and the ride smoothed out. Soon the big pecan trees at the Sheridan headquarters came into sight, then the corrals and ranch buildings. Chase drove past them all as if he did it every day, then steered the pickup onto the lawn behind her house and drove across the stone patio to the back door, turning sharply at the last moment to position the passenger door of the truck closer to the house before he stopped and switched off the engine.

The windshield wipers stopped with the engine, and Fay saw it was only sprinkling here. The wind was gusting hard as she got her door open and tried to get out of the pickup before Chase could come around and help her. She'd barely got her feet out before Chase surged close and plucked her off the seat to carry her to the door.

Good thing he didn't need her to put her arms around his neck, because he'd trapped her right arm behind him and she couldn't lift her injured left one high enough to reach his shoulder. As soon as they were in the mudroom, he kicked the door closed to tromp into the silent kitchen, bellowing as he did.

"Margie? You still here?"

The shout startled Fay and she jerked in his arms, setting off every ache in her body. She barely managed to stifle a moan and tried to cover it with a quick, "She's gone. Put me down."

Her order didn't slow Chase in the least as he walked into the hall then into the living room to sit her on the sofa. He left her briefly to grab the TV remote, switch it on, then surf through the channels to find weather coverage.

While his back was turned, Fay fought her way to her feet despite the dizziness that swamped her. Her head was pounding and her legs felt alarmingly weak, but she managed a couple of unsteady steps before Chase found a local weather bulletin and turned back to her.

"Sit down and let me see what's hurt," he said gruffly as he eased her back toward the sofa. "As soon as we see how bad the storm is between here and Coulter City, we'll go to the hospital."

Fay managed to pull from his grip, thankful it was her good arm he'd caught. "I don't need a hospital."

"The hell you don't," he growled. "You're white as a sheet and movin' like you're a hundred years old. An' you gotta knot the size of a goose egg in your hair."

That last remark was accompanied by

the feel of his big fingers lightly grazing her hair, and the shower of tingles that produced was alarming.

"I'm fine, just a little stiff," she said, trying to sound steadier than she felt. "Nothing that can't be fixed with a hot shower and an ice pack."

Chase's answer to that was to bend down and pick her up again. Her pained intake of breath made him go still for a moment before he turned to walk to the hall stairs.

"I reckon a fast shower and some dry clothes wouldn't hurt," he allowed, "but the hospital's a must once the storm passes."

Frustration sent little nettles through her, the perfect accompaniment to the aching protest her body was making. At least the trip up the stairs was more tolerable than she'd anticipated—and a whole lot easier than going up them under her own power—but she hated being treated like an invalid.

Since the house was almost dark from the late afternoon storm, Chase paused at the top of the stairs to switch on the hall lights before he strode on to the master bedroom. It was her bedroom, and of course he knew where it was, thanks to Margie's desperation all those months ago. He walked straight to the bathroom and flipped on the light in there.

Fay could hardly wait for him to put her down and leave. Once he did, she'd lock the door and have a good long soak in the tub. Short of breaking down the door, Chase would have to go away. Eventually. He sat her down, then bent to take off her boots.

She bit her lip at the added pain that caused, though it was obvious Chase had tried to be gentle.

"Okay, thanks," she said when he'd set her boots aside.

Chase straightened and glared down at her. For the first time, Fay allowed herself to look directly into his face and meet his blue gaze.

Chase Rafferty was a man's man, big, wide-shouldered, his lean, thick-muscled build made powerful by hard work. It was a long way for her to look up and it hurt to do it now. She tried not to notice for the millionth time that he wasn't classically handsome, that his kind of handsomeness was the rugged, enduring kind. The man would still be making heads turn and hearts skip at ninety, and she was glad she'd lost interest.

"I can take care of things from here," she told him. "The worst of the storm should pass soon, maybe before I'm even done in here, so you can go on home."

It wasn't a subtle hint to clear out ASAP, and Chase's response wasn't subtle, either.

"I'm not goin' anywhere till I take you to town. There's too much lightning for anything but a quick shower, so let's do

3something about those clothes. You're soaked through."

He started to lean down again, but she held up a shaky hand to ward him off.

"I can undress myself," she insisted, in no mood to allow that. She was neither feeble nor helpless. "Wait outside the door if you must, but leave."

Chase was still leaning down, so she added, "And check the weather. For all we know, that funnel cloud touched down and is on its way here."

"You've still got lights," he pointed out, but he straightened, finally getting the message that she could take care of herself. "I'll be close if you get into trouble."

Guilt over her bad manners was the only thing that kept her from being more rude than she'd already been. That and the fact that he was finally going away.

"Fine."

"Fine," he mocked, though his blue eyes were burning sternly into hers, as if he was trying to discern how capable she really was of taking care of herself once she was alone.

He must have decided she could handle things herself, because he moved to the door. He turned to pull it shut on his way out before he paused.

"Don't lock this." The emphasis was on don't, and she felt her last nerve snap.

"Don't tell me what to do in my own house," she said hotly, and what passed for a faint smile sneaked over his stern mouth before he closed the door.

CHAPTER TWO

ABOUT five seconds after she'd wrestled off her jeans and dropped them next to the tub, Fay remembered the sorrel.

She never neglected her animals, *never,* just as she never exposed them to foolish risks. The fact that she'd done both to the sorrel today made her queasy with remorse. Her foolishness with the storm had surely broken the horse's trust, and it shamed her to realize she had no idea if he'd made it back to the stable or if he was still loose, or worse, injured.

Appalled at herself, Fay moved gingerly to the bathroom door and opened it a crack to look out into her bedroom. Chase was standing at the window, his back to her as he stared out at the storm. It had arrived at the headquarters full force, and the bedroom windows were gray with rain. The blur of movement beyond the glass was because the branches of the big shade trees out back were rocking in the wind.

Chase had the bedroom extension phone in his hand, but she couldn't hear what he was saying. When he hung up, Fay called out.

"Would you mind handing me the phone? I need to call the stable office."

Chase turned toward her. "I just did. Riley said to tell you the sorrel's back. He came in just before they saw my truck go by."

"Then he's okay?"

"Far as Riley could tell."

The somber way he said it shamed her for putting the horse at risk in the first place, and her guilt multiplied. She retreated a little more behind the door and hastily changed the subject.

"If the storm doesn't let up soon, help yourself to coffee downstairs. It's fresh made, but in the thermos."

She didn't tell him about the hot food Margie would have left in the oven because she hoped he wouldn't be here long enough to eat. That's when she remembered he'd gotten wet, too. "Help yourself to a towel in the downstairs bathroom," she added. "There might be a dry T-shirt in the laundry room that'll fit. Or toss your shirt in the drier for a few minutes."

Fay closed the door, relieved to shut him out and shut out the subject of the sorrel. At least she'd bossed him enough to demonstrate she was anything but a candidate for the emergency room, but as she finished undressing, she realized how weak she was.

Reddish-purple bruises already marked her shoulder, hip, and outer thigh. They'd be worse tomorrow, but she'd had bruises before so she wasn't impressed. It was the headache and the growing muscle aches beneath the bruises that would cause the most inconvenience.

Fay stepped carefully into the shower and drew the curtain. Her hands trembled a little as she twisted on the faucets and adjusted the temperature. Hampered by her aching shoulder and arm, she clumsily soaped and rinsed, then washed her hair before she stood under the jet of hot water and let the heat soothe her neck, shoulder and hip for a few moments.

Dizziness made her give up on daring a long soak in the tub, so she turned off the water and reached for a towel to dry off. She did what she could about drying her hair with another towel, careful of the painful lump on the side of her head.

Finally she wrapped up in a robe and opened the door to peek into the bedroom.

Chase was gone. As she hobbled out, she could hear the increasing intensity of the storm, not surprised to see that the trees outside her window were swaying harder in the unnatural darkness. Hail pounded the roof and some of it pelted the glass.

It aggravated her to get dressed again, but there was no way she could go downstairs in a robe while Chase was here. She collected a few clothes and stepped back into the bathroom to dress in privacy. After a pulling on fresh underwear, jeans and a baggy cotton shirt to conceal the fact that her arm and shoulder were too sore to manage a bra, she felt worn-out.

It was probably hunger and fatigue more than the fall that made her weak, and maybe the strong emotion at the boundary fence played a part in her weariness now. Since she'd feel better with dry hair, she reached for the blow drier. It was a good thing she was wearing her hair short these days because the small chore was as painful as it was awkward.

By the time she was finished, the sounds of the storm had eased. With any luck, she'd be able to get rid of Chase soon, but the idea failed to revive her. In fact, she felt strangely let down.

A sudden neediness went through her, bringing back the memory of hearing her brothers' voices. She still didn't understand those moments by the boundary fence, but the sudden craving to catch at least a wisp of that familiar, otherworldly touch was a potent lure, and tempted her to slip down the hall to their room.

Though she felt drained, the moment she walked out of the bathroom and saw Chase sitting on the bench at the foot of her bed, she scrambled to conceal it. His shirt looked dry, he'd taken off his Stetson, and there was something about the sight of him relaxing next to her bed made her insides go warm.

He looked far too natural—and appealing—in her private space, and the strong sense that a line between them was about to be crossed sent a flutter of panic through her. A year ago, she would have been wild with joy…

Chase stood. "Everything all right?"

The question set off a spark of resentment. Nothing was right, and hadn't been for a long time. Things might never be right again, and the fact that he'd asked—and that he was still here—doubled her sense that nothing would ever be right again.

Fay realized she was overreacting. Guilt over the sorrel and her automatic hostility toward Chase swam into the mix of exhaustion and agitated emotions to make her feel edgy and raw. If she could just get rid of him, she could have a hot meal and an early bedtime.

"I'm fine," she said, unable to sound even marginally polite.

Chase's gaze drilled skeptically into hers, then shifted to the side of her head as if he were searching for evidence of the painful swelling. The fact that his gaze checked the angle of her injured left shoulder then softened to move lingeringly down her chest to her waist before he took in the way she was favoring her left leg, sent a rash of feminine self-consciousness through her that gave her nerves another hard stir.

"Now's a good time to get to town."

"I'm not going to town," she said tersely, shoving down the guilt she'd felt mere seconds ago.

He gave a solemn nod. "So you're gonna tough it out, huh?"

"Yup." She started across the room and into the hall to the back stairs, moving as normally as she could, but her left hip and knee were stiff enough to keep her stride short and uneven. At least she could walk, and she was never more grateful than now for her natural vigor and resilience.

"Maybe a hefty share of toughness comes in handy for a plan like yours," he commented, and she rose to the bait before she could catch herself.

"What plan?"

"The plan to do yourself in."

The blunt words made her falter and lose her balance just enough to step wrong. Her hip and knee gave out and she grabbed wildly for the wall. The sudden move sent agony through her strained muscles, but Chase caught her waist and kept her from falling.

"Damn, Fay," he swore as she panted hard to keep a cry back, "that had to hurt."

Oh, it did! Her lashes were wet, and she bit her lip as she waited for the pain to settle down. And then the gentle mockery in his gruff tone registered.

He must have been able to tell when it did, because he chuckled grimly. "Successful or not, I'd guess pain's the biggest drawback of doing yourself in. You gotta be tough to face that."

The outrageous comment startled a laugh out of her before temper roared up to stifle it. "I did *not* plan to do myself… in," she panted, seizing the flimsy defense. She hadn't *planned.*

"Glad to hear it, you bein' so young and all. Your brothers woulda had a fit."

The mention of her brothers made her see red and a fresh flood of ire rushed up, dulling the pain that gripped her.

"Don't you dare—" she strained to turn enough to look him in the eye "—tell me what my brothers would have said." That was the moment the memory of hearing their voices at the fence surged back.

No, Fay, run! Don't do it!

Of all the things Chase might have said…

* * *

Chase looked down into fiery blue eyes a couple shades darker than his own, and felt a spark of satisfaction. Getting her anger into the open was better than letting it bubble inside and drive her to do crazy things. And clichéd as it was, she was beautiful when she was angry. That flare of temper had burned away the dullness in her eyes and sent a wild flush to her face. But he didn't want her to hate him.

"I apologize, Miss Fay," he said, meaning it. "I meant no disrespect to your brothers, or to your memory of them." He searched her fiery gaze, hoping he could get past the anger he'd deliberately provoked and get her to listen. "But I did mean to shake you up and make you think. What you did out there wasn't like you."

He saw the tears that had sprung into all that fire after his mention of Ty and Troy, and he felt pity for the heavy grief she still carried. How she'd endured it this long alone was a testament to her strength, but it was time for her to get past the worst of it. She was too young and vital to stay cut off from life and locked into this kind of hurt. And then she surprised him. Her voice was husky and a little choked.

"You're welcome to share supper. Margie always leaves more than enough for one."

The tension he'd felt began to ease. "Thanks."

She looked away from him. The invitation to share supper must mean she'd forgiven him for using her brothers to get through to her about today. Or maybe she was just repaying him for his help. But the way she straightened, casually managing to move his hands away from her waist, let him know the subject of doing herself in was closed.

He'd be glad to let it be closed, if today was really the end of it. He'd pushed—

maybe too much—but she hadn't told him to leave. Ironically, now that he'd said something that probably ought to get him thrown out, she'd invited him to stay.

The extra irony was that he wasn't sure why he'd been so hell-bent to keep poking into her life when she treated him with about the same enthusiasm she would have given someone who'd tracked in something smelly from the barn. And yet what had started out as neighborly concern had turned into a challenge he hadn't been able to leave alone. Maybe Fay wasn't the only one who needed to look at what she'd done and think.

When they reached the kitchen, Fay had little choice but to allow it when Chase took over getting the food from the warming oven. As she'd said, Margie had made more than enough for one, and tonight it was a large meat and pasta casserole in a heavy glass dish. Two vegetable salads in the refrigerator, one sweet and one tangy, completed the meal. Fay took down an extra place setting to add to the one Margie had left on a tray for her, but Chase carried it to the table.

As she got out a bottle of analgesic and took two tablets, Fay watched Chase set the table and open the thermos to pour coffee. He'd never seemed very domesticated to her, so it was interesting to see him managing the small kitchen tasks with only a little awkwardness.

Fay sat down across the table from him, bracing her good hand on the edge of the tabletop to ease herself down. It was all she could do to keep from showing how much it hurt to bend her body, but she was desperate to sit. She was light-headed and her knees were shaking. The confrontation upstairs had drained her even more but she felt an odd peace inside, as if a dam had broken relieving her of some nameless pressure.

"I could've helped you sit down," Chase said as he finished with the coffee and pulled out his chair.

"I've been sitting down without help most of my life," she said as she pulled the napkin from beneath her silverware and dropped it onto her lap.

He didn't respond to that as he used the metal spatula to cut a generous square of casserole from the pan and put it on her plate. She mumbled a soft thanks and started eating. She'd been ravenous, and the more she ate, the better she began to feel.

Neither of them spoke while they ate, which in both their cases was habit. Their work was physically demanding and the days were long, so at mealtimes food was the priority. Talk came later, and she was both relieved and wary. Relieved because the talk she'd dreaded had already come in the upstairs hall, wary because she didn't know what else they could possibly talk about.

The resentment she'd felt toward Chase these past months, particularly today, was gone, and having him at her table was starting to affect her. She'd hated eating alone here, and rarely had the past year. She hadn't been able to bear seeing the boys' empty places, so she either ate at the kitchen counter or fixed a tray of food and took it with her to the den to do paperwork. Tonight it felt almost pleasant to sit here, in spite of the circumstances and the company.

Her heart cautiously tested that as she glanced toward Ty and Troy's empty chairs. The ache she expected was soft instead of sharp, and she glanced briefly across the table at Chase before she looked down at her plate to finish her meal. Was it because someone shared the table with her, or was it because that someone was Chase?

"You've got color in your cheeks," Chase commented as he sat back with his coffee. Fay set her fork down, and reached for her own coffee.

"I was starved."

"You've got a healthy appetite. That's a good sign."

"Stop looking for signs," she told him. "I've got nothing more than a bump on the head, strained muscles and some colorful bruises. Been there, done that, and so have you."

"Have you got someone who can stay the night?"

"I don't need a baby-sitter," she scoffed as she set her napkin next to her plate.

"Head injuries are nothing to mess with."

"I'll be fine."

She'd made that sound neutral, but she suddenly didn't know how to handle his persistence. It made her realize she'd kept him at bay with irritation and resentment and sarcasm so long that she wasn't sure how to deal with him any other way, which was why she had a hard time being polite to him, even now.

The silence went on for several moments, long enough to renew her hope that he'd go home.

"Think you can make it up to bed under your own power?" The question meant he'd leave soon, but the relief she'd expected didn't come.

"I want to watch TV a while. I might even sleep down here. Sometimes the recliner's more comfortable than lying flat." There. She could speak to him in a more friendly tone, but she started to regret giving him the small encouragement when he went on.

"I still don't think it's a good idea for you to be alone, and there'll be more storms. You might have to go to your storm room, and there's always the chance you'll start to feel worse."

"I'll know what to do," she said, trying not to make that sound too grouchy. In other circumstances and with someone else, it might have been amusing to see Chase Rafferty play mother hen.

"Knowin' and doin' are two different things," he pointed out as he stood. "I'll tidy up for you," he added before she could object, and she watched as he stacked their things on the tray and carried them to the dishwasher.

He opened the door, pulled out the rack and efficiently loaded it. He apparently knew his way around a dishwasher, but it was a machine. Ty and Troy hadn't minded getting stuck with dishwasher duty, declaring that loading the dishwasher was the only halfway manly job in the kitchen.

The sudden memory didn't hurt as much as she'd expected, and that got her attention, but the absence of painful grief suddenly felt disloyal, and guilt followed swiftly to send her heart low…

Chase's soft question so close to her ear startled her. "Are you fallin' asleep?"

She'd been so lost in private misery these past moments that she hadn't noticed him finish clearing the table and walk back to her.

The words, "I'm fine," babbled out like the automatic response they'd become.

"I asked if you were falling asleep," he said with a chuckle. "Yes? No?"

"No."

In truth, she'd lapsed into one of those long, long moments that could so easily become hours when she was by herself. Thankfully Chase didn't seem to realize it.

"Let's see how well you can get up and move around on your own."

Fay reached for the table edge and tried to unbend enough to stand, but she was so stiff now that she couldn't get much more than a couple inches off the chair before she had to sit back down. Frustration made her try again. Though she got only a little higher than before, Chase gently helped her unbend enough to stand reasonably straight.

"I saw liniment in your downstairs bathroom. While you rub some on, I'll move my truck and make an ice pack for that knot on your head."

Fay didn't reply to that because she was trying to adjust to the stiff pain that seemed to have locked up every muscle. Movement would loosen them, so she turned carefully from the table and walked across the kitchen into the back hall that led to the bathroom. By the time she got there, she was a lot more limber, but it took some doing to get her jeans down and make use of the liniment. Once she was finished, she walked out and made her way to the living room.

The TV was still on and she made a

partial circuit around the room to walk off a little more stiffness before she gingerly lowered herself onto one of the two recliners and struggled to ease it back. Chase brought in the ice pack, coffee Thermos and their cups and she noticed a few dapples of rain on his shoulders and in his hair.

"You've got some small branches down from the first blow-through," he told her. "Nothing major."

He set her coffee on the table next to her chair, handed her the waterproof cloth pouch he'd filled with ice, then sat down in the second recliner with his coffee cup. He looked for all the world as if he was settling in, and Fay felt her resistance to that idea waver as she placed the ice pouch against the side of her head.

How many women in their part of Texas would have loved to have Chase Rafferty around, waiting on them? Maybe it would be less aggravating to look at it that way.

It would certainly take less energy than trying to get rid of him.

And from the sounds of it, a new storm was blowing in, so it might not be the smartest thing for him to leave and have it break before he could get home. Yes, he'd lived in these parts all of his life and had weathered dozens of bad storms, just as she had. They both were accustomed to the dangers and knew how to handle them, but it would be churlish to send him home at the wrong time.

Besides, she couldn't help noticing that it felt comfortable to sit in her living room with company. Though she'd been too grouchy to convey much more than a speck of hospitality, Chase seemed immune to her bad mood. Now that he'd stopped bossing her and asking nosy questions, she decided she almost liked that he was here. It was a bonus that he didn't seem inclined to make small talk. In fact, the silence between them was almost companionable, and that was as soothing to her as it was surprising.

Chase used the TV remote to switch to a local channel that had interrupted regular programming to show the progress of the storms before he offered her the remote. She waved it away, and he set it within her easy reach.

Fay felt her body sink further into the cushy recliner, and exhaustion began to roll over her in waves. Between the hot, filling meal, the analgesic and the liniment, the sharp edges of her various aches and pains had been dulled. The chair put her in a physical position that was more comfortable than she could have hoped for, and suddenly her eyelids felt as if they weighed a pound apiece. An alien sense of well-being came in on the next wave of exhaustion and she was asleep before she could make sense of it.

CHAPTER THREE

SOUNDS from the kitchen began to bring Fay around that next morning. Her first thought was that Margie must be having it out with a frying pan. Her position in the recliner began to register, and she realized the reason she could hear Margie in the kitchen was because she'd slept in the recliner all night.

The TV was set on a network morning show, but the volume was low enough to provide a pleasant drone of voices. An afghan from the cabinet behind the sofa covered her from chin to foot and she snuggled deeper into the fleecy warmth before the pain of moving brought her fully awake.

Her head began to pound again as she leaned to the side to reach for the lever that put the chair into its sitting position. Her gaze automatically went to the other recliner, but it sat empty. Chase was gone, and his absence was a surprising letdown that made all her aches and pains feel worse.

Another day stretched impossibly long before her, a day to fill up so she couldn't dwell on the boys, only today she'd have the added challenge of pushing a hurting body to get things done. As she struggled to her feet and slowly tried to unbend enough to stand straight, she felt hollow inside, and suddenly felt so bleak that tears surged behind her eyes.

It had been months since she'd awakened feeling weepy, and the idea that she was losing ground was disheartening. She gritted her teeth against the pain and the weepy feelings and dredged up the will to move toward the back hall and the bathroom.

Because she was still so stiff, dashing her face with cold water splattered more around than she'd meant to, and she ended up leaning against the cabinet with a hand braced on the countertop. She felt herself slipping back into the black depression she'd worked so hard to escape, and made the huge effort it took to shove aside self-pity and reach for a towel to blot her face.

She would *not* give in to this, she vowed as she wiped up the water spills around the sink. As if to thwart her vow, a chill breath of anxiety quivered through her the instant before a panic attack came on her full force. The room was closing in, and she abruptly turned and fumbled open the door to flee. Once in the hall she expected to feel better, but the panic wrenched higher and she hobbled toward the mudroom. What was wrong with her?

With shaking hands, she grabbed a pair of sandals out of a cubbyhole of old shoes, dropped them to the floor and slid her feet into them. The mysterious panic that had electrified her insides drove her out the back door to the patio and she started across the flat stones, moving past the scattered leaves and small branches the storm had taken down.

She felt out of control, and the desperate need to drive the confusing feelings away made her push herself in an instinctive need to outrun the panic. Until yesterday, she'd been immune to fear. Now it was choking her.

Fay labored to the side of the patio and shifted directions to walk through the wet grass to the lane that circled the house. She didn't want anyone to see her like this, so the front driveway that led to the highway a mile away was the perfect place to walk off the panic and loosen her strained muscles.

The moment she made it around the house, Fay saw Chase's white pickup parked out front. Had he come back? A small tree branch had blown down and rested across the hood of the truck, and from the looks of the ground the vehicle hadn't been moved all night. That meant Chase was still here, but instead of feeling angry about it Fay felt her panic magically begin to level off, then to ease.

The relief she felt was as mysterious as the reason the sudden panic had come in the first place. *Was she losing her mind?* The repeated question brought one more surge of panic before the baffling fear again began to calm. A heartbeat later she was startled by the low voice that called out behind her.

"What're you doing out here?"

Fay stiffly glanced back to see Chase walking after her. He'd spent the night in his clothes, but he looked wonderfully unrumpled. His dark hair had a healthy, inviting shine in the early light and he had a very macho show of beard stubble that made him look like an outlaw. Men like him would need to shave a little more than once a day, and she appreciated even more that he managed to look clean-shaven most of the times she'd seen him. His eyes, so blue in a deeply tanned face, held her gaze and magically transmitted a warmth that soothed away the lingering chill of panic.

He apparently accepted her soft, "I needed to walk off some stiffness," because he nodded.

"Miss Margie says to tell you there's a coffee cake in the oven," he said as they walked along the lane to the stone path that would lead around the other side of the house and return them to the patio. "And just so you'll have some warning, Margie didn't approve of me spending the night."

Knowing Margie, the news wasn't unexpected. It still amazed Fay that Margie had once allowed Chase to come upstairs to beat on her bedroom door to wake her up. On the other hand, she could bet Margie had been standing nearby to make certain the door stayed shut, though back then Fay had been in such bad shape emotionally that Margie might have allowed most anything.

"Well, now you've done it," she said, a little pleased that he'd fallen out of favor with her housekeeper. "Did she get out a shotgun?"

"Said she's worried about what the men'll think."

"If they even knew you'd stayed. You moved your truck to the front driveway. They couldn't have seen it from the bunkhouse."

Chase shook his head. "After you went to sleep, we had a storm bad enough that I almost woke you up. Riley was out checking around the headquarters after it passed, saw the truck and came knockin' at the door. He was about as glad to see me as you always are, and then Miss Margie got here earlier than usual this morning, or so she said. Riley must have called her."

A rare tickle of amusement made her smile. She could point out that this was the consequence of sticking his nose in where it didn't belong, but he'd helped her yesterday so she couldn't do it. Instead she said, "You know what they say, 'No good deed goes unpunished.'"

They reached the back door and Chase opened it for her to go in. She nudged her sandals off in the mudroom and while Chase scuffed his boots dry on a mat, she went ahead of him into the kitchen. She washed her hands at the sink, knowing that Margie watched her every move. When she dried off and turned, Margie confronted her.

"How come you didn't call me last night if you needed somebody to stay with you? You know I would have come back, bad weather or not."

"I didn't need you to come back. I was—"

"How bad is that knock on the noggin?" Margie stepped close and reached up to briefly feel the size of the lump. The spot was still tender. "You need to be in bed, not hobbling around outside," Margie declared. "After you eat a good breakfast, you can rest another hour or two in the chair before I call the doctor's office to get you seen."

"I don't need to see a doctor," Fay said, moving around the small, feisty woman to make her way to the table. Chase followed and chivalrously helped her sit.

"The whole neighborhood'll be talkin'," Margie huffed as she began bringing food to the table.

"I doubt that," Fay said as she reached for her napkin.

Once Margie set the platter of bacon and sausage, and the bowl of fried potato chunks between them, she shot Chase a glare before she went back to grab the egg skillet off the stove. At the table, she slid four over-easy eggs onto each of their plates then gave them both a no-nonsense look.

"The two of you'd better decide what your intentions are from here on. Folks are too casual about those kinda things these days."

Surprised and a little embarrassed, Fay looked over at Margie. Was she joking?

"We didn't do a thing we wouldn't have done if you'd been in the room," Fay assured her.

"Maybe not this time. But what about the way you've been?"

Fay saw the sudden discomfort in

Margie's stern expression and automatically braced herself for what was coming.

"This past year's been hard on you. A man like Mr. Rafferty comes along and there's no tellin' what you might take it in your head to do."

Fay felt heat scorch across her cheeks and glanced over at Chase, mortified as Margie charged on.

"And no offense to Mr. Rafferty, but he's still sowin' his wild oats. Probably not even thinking about marriage yet."

Fay got out a cringing, "Margie, I appreciate your concern, but—"

"You know we all worry about you, Miss Fay." Now Margie reached out and gently touched Fay's short hair in silent apology before she pulled her hand back and changed the subject. "I'm washing clothes this morning. Thought I'd get the first load hung outside before it gets too hot, and the washer's almost through its cycle. You know how you like your work clothes line-dried." She gave Chase another glare. "I'll check on you later."

With that, Margie turned away and marched to the laundry room, the smart rap of her shoes underscoring her promise to return. Fay lifted her napkin to her mouth and pressed hard, torn between laughter and acute embarrassment. Margie hadn't been kidding, and it was to Chase's credit that he'd put up with it all without a word.

"I guess we might as well talk to the preacher."

Chase's sober statement sent a fresh shock through her system and her eyes widened. "Wh-what?"

"Marrying you might give Miss Margie a better opinion of me. And you might like having a husband to crab at."

Fay lowered her napkin, her amusement gone. "Very funny."

She dropped the napkin to her lap and

picked up her fork. The over-easy eggs had gone cold so Fay mashed them up and spooned some of the hot potato chunks over the mix and dug in, certain she'd heard the last of Chase's poor attempt at humor.

After several minutes while the only sounds in the house came from the laundry room down the hall and the occasional chink of silverware on china, Chase reached for his coffee, had a sip, then gave her a solemn look.

"Have you put in writing what you want for Sheridan Ranch if something happens to you? If you'd died out at the fence yesterday, or been hurt enough not to be able to run things long-term, what then? Have you got a will?"

The out of the blue question was as stunning and bizarre as everything else was turning out to be that morning, and it irritated Fay to no end. "Butt out," she grumbled, but Chase ignored the order.

"Normally I wouldn't think about it." *But after you tried to kill yourself in the storm yesterday…*

Though he hadn't said the words, they were the subtext, and Fay felt her face flush again, only with anger this time.

"So you still want to lease land from Sheridan," she guessed, and it was more a statement than a question. He'd mentioned leasing at least twice in the past year, so it was a natural conclusion. And it made sense that if Chase wanted to work out a deal with her, he'd want some assurance that the land wouldn't be tied up in probate if she suddenly died without a will.

"I'm still thinking about it," he allowed, "along with what happened yesterday afternoon. Then there's the marriage idea, thanks to Miss Margie. The more I think about that, the more sense it makes. Marriage could tidy up a lot of things for us."

Fay stared in disbelief. One corner of

his mouth quirked, sending the signal he was about to say something even more outrageous.

"Then there's the pleasure side of marriage, the one Miss Margie's worried we'll take prematurely. Problems solved all the way around."

Fay's brain froze to a halt in the middle of "the pleasure side of marriage," and she realized belatedly that she needed to take a breath. When she was able to speak, she sounded as if she was still breathless. "You can't be serious."

"Think about it till you feel better," he said reasonably, and Fay gave her head a faint shake. "I'll come around in a few days, see what your answer is." He went back to his food as casually as if he'd commented on the weather while she was so shocked she was dizzy.

Maybe she *did* need to lie down, and maybe she needed to see a doctor after all.

The world had tilted a little off its axis, though for once in a very long time, the way it had tilted didn't cause pain, just… consternation.

She realized then that the dark menace of depression that had reared its ugly head that morning was long gone. Not sure what that meant, she mentally searched for any wisp of it or her earlier panic, but neither torment remained. The oven buzzer went off and while Margie bustled in to take the coffee cake out of the oven, Fay continued to explore these new feelings.

The day that had seemed so endless and empty earlier suddenly felt brighter, almost promising. She'd forgotten what it felt like to look forward to anything, much less a new day. When she noticed that Margie's sternness with them had markedly eased by the time she brought the coffee cake to the table, the day brightened a little more.

"I 'bout forgot this," Margie said. "It's a new recipe, so save me a piece."

Fay was amazed that the woman's normal, chatty friendliness had been restored. It was as if the earlier confrontation had never happened. Margie even rested her hand briefly on Chase's shoulder as she leaned in to refill his coffee cup before she came around the table to top off Fay's. Had she overheard Chase mention marriage?

"If you wouldn't mind cutting up that coffee cake, Mr. Rafferty, I can get done in the laundry room and get Fay's things on the clothesline." At his nod, Margie set the coffee carafe on a brass trivet near his plate before she left the kitchen.

Fay sank back in her chair, trying to cope with the emotional whiplash Margie had just dealt them. She looked over helplessly at Chase and a surprising burst of good humor almost gurgled out. "I don't know what to say."

Chase's dark brows had come together in a frown. "Women like your Miss Margie confuse the heck outta us men," he said darkly. "Are you ready for a slice of this?" he asked as he picked up the knife and held it over the coffee cake.

It was after 9:00 a.m. before Fay escaped the house to check on the sorrel. Chase had gone home after breakfast, and Margie finally gave up trying to get her to rest. Fay had flatly refused to see a doctor, and once Margie had gone upstairs to dust, she'd taken the opportunity to slip out the back door with a broom.

The leaves and small branches she'd seen earlier needed to be stacked for disposal, and she meant to take care of at least that much on her way to the stable. If not for the dull headache she still had and her stiff muscles, she could have picked them up and carried them with her to be disposed of, but using the broom to whisk them out of the way into a pile would have to do.

The sorrel whickered a greeting the moment she stepped into the stable. He was waiting for her, eagerly bobbing his head over the stall gate as she approached.

"Hey, there, Billy," she crooned as she gave his big head an apologetic rub. As she lifted the halter, he bent his neck to accommodate her clumsy effort to buckle it and clip on a lead rope. Fay opened the gate and stood aside as he pranced into the stable aisle.

He was obviously eager to get out into the sunshine, so she led him to a corral. Once they were inside and the gate was closed, Fay forced her strained muscles to cooperate as she leaned down to run her hands over his legs and check his hooves.

Though her body protested and her head pounded, she had to see for herself that the horse hadn't been injured by her foolishness. Billy turned his head to nibble playfully at the loose hem of her shirt as if to chide her for not tucking it in like she usually did. At her gentle scolding, he stopped, gave a long, relaxed snort and continued to stand patiently.

By the time she slowly straightened, cold sweat beaded her face and she leaned weakly against the sorrel's sleek side. After a few moments, she moved to his head, unclipped the lead rope and signaled him to move forward.

Billy minced away and she gave the end of the lead rope a twirl. The sorrel, ever attentive to her, began to circle the corral. Fay turned to keep her eyes on him, watching for any hint of lameness or muscle strain, but the big horse performed perfectly, even taking a moment to show off when he bucked and then increased his pace around the pen. Fay stopped twirling the end of the rope and the horse angled away from the rails to come to her.

This time, he boldly nuzzled her jeans' pocket before he lipped the tail of her shirt and gave it a tug. Fay smiled wearily and dug out the bits of carrot she'd swiped from the refrigerator. Billy neatly plucked the first piece off her palm and munched it enthusiastically. He shadowed her as she started for the gate, giving her arm a playful nudge to coax another treat. When they reached the gate, Fay removed his halter and fed him the rest before she lifted the gate latch and left him in the partially shaded corral.

About that time, Riley rode into the main alley between the network of corrals, saw her and called out a greeting. Fay hung the halter and lead rope on the gatepost as Riley rode up. He nodded toward Billy.

"There's not a thing wrong with that

horse, except he'd like to be out doing his job." Riley dismounted and gave her a serious look. "Unlike you," he pointed out bluntly. "You ought not be out here in this heat, Miss Fay. You're lookin' mighty puny."

"Just having a look around," she said, feeling more than "puny" by now. The sun was hot enough to make her feel light-headed, and she sorely regretted leaving her hat at the house. Like it or not, she was done in and had no choice but to go back to the house and rest.

"Why don't you let me walk you back?" Riley said, gently taking her elbow to start her back to the stable. He left his horse in the stable aisle and they walked on through to the other doors. "I rode out to where Rafferty said you'd taken the fall, but he's already got a crew out there."

Fay couldn't make sense of that bit of information. "What's that?" she asked, grateful to be out of the sun during the brief time it took for them to walk through the stable.

"Seems he drove through the fence yesterday when Billy tossed you off, so he's having it fixed. I checked the cattle over that way, and cut out a few R/K cows to run 'em back on Rafferty's side. His boys'll have the fence done pretty quick."

There was an awkward tension about Riley that she finally noticed as they stepped out of the stable and into the sun again, and that made her remember Margie's worry about what the men would think of Chase staying overnight. She didn't expect Riley to say anything about it—even if it had bothered him, which she doubted—but she sensed his concern about something. He didn't keep her guessing.

"I didn't realize you were so far from the house when that storm blew up yesterday," he said, his voice a little gruff. "Maybe you were trying to finish up your work and time got away from you, but..."

Fay felt a twist of shame. Though Riley was trying to put a good face on it, she got the message anyway. Somehow he knew she'd taken a foolish chance with her life, and that she'd done it on purpose. Had Chase blabbed his theory to him or had he only mentioned what had happened and Riley had drawn his own conclusion?

It rattled her to think that Riley had figured it out on his own. It made her wonder what she'd been doing this past year that would give him the idea, though the truth was, she'd been so wrapped in misery that she hadn't given much thought to how she looked to others.

Thankfully they reached the back patio and the urge to explain away yesterday was cut short. She couldn't admit to her foreman that she'd had a crazy few moments and briefly given in to a self-destructive impulse, so there was nothing to say unless she wanted to lie.

"I'll take care of those branches," Riley said. "All the men haven't reported in yet, but I think we lucked out over here. Rafferty's fence crew said the R/K lost a couple of outbuildings and had some window and roof damage at the main house."

Fay murmured a quiet thanks as he opened the door for her and she went inside.

Margie was still upstairs, so Fay took a moment to wash up before she headed for the living room. Her legs finally gave out as she was bending to sit and she dropped painfully onto the recliner. She had just enough energy left to tilt the chair back and cover up with the afghan.

Her lashes dropped heavily shut as she began to relax. So Chase's place had sustained some damage while he'd been over here last night baby-sitting her. He'd probably be tied up with insurance filings and getting supplies together for repairs and replacement buildings, so he'd be too busy to butt into her life for a while.

She ignored the faint touch of disappointment that caused, and drifted quickly to sleep.

CHAPTER FOUR

FAY slept through the noon meal and woke up at 2:00 p.m. Margie brought her a tray of small sandwiches, a glass of milk and a wedge of pecan pie to tide her over till supper. She felt worlds better after a good nap and a meal, but without the distraction of work, the events of that morning began to replay in her mind.

Had Chase really suggested they get married? Now that it had come to mind again, she realized that the second time he'd mentioned it, he'd sounded serious. It was hardly the proposal she'd hoped to receive one day, but there was an odd appeal to it. Before Ty and Troy had been killed, she'd had the same storybook fantasy most girls do about falling in love and getting married, but that had changed. Falling in love was the last thing she wanted now.

But a marriage based on business might not be so bad, and she owed it to her family to keep Sheridan Ranch going. None of her cousins would be interested in that, but someone like Chase Rafferty would. He lived and breathed ranching and everything that went with it, the more challenging the better.

His Rafferty/Keenan Ranch had been formed over a business deal between two families in the 1940s, with both family names preserved. If something happened to her, the Sheridan name could be preserved with the land, and that made the idea more attractive. She was well into plans for just such a marriage arrangement when she brought herself up short.

Chase hadn't been serious, he couldn't have been. Besides, he'd mentioned the pleasure side of marriage. That part held no attraction for her at all, not when it produced babies. After losing the boys, she was more than a little terrified of losing a child of her own, so some form of birth control was a must. On the other hand, it might take years to work up the courage to have a child, so was it safe to be on the pill that long?

Fay suddenly realized she'd stopped thinking about marrying Chase and had instead lapsed into thinking about sex with Chase. Not thinking about what it might actually be like to *have* sex with him, thank heavens, but about having sex often enough to worry about birth control. It was reassuring to discover that her brain was just as closed to dwelling on what sex with Chase might be like as it was to falling in love with him, but she was practical enough to realize that there might be sex from time to time, even in a business marriage.

Her mind was just starting to veer into a reminder that having loveless sex was almost as unappealing to her as the risk of pregnancy, when she again brought herself up short. Irritated, and determined to stop dwelling on anything to do with marriage, Fay abandoned the recliner and braved the stairs to her bedroom. Once she reached the top she realized that compared to the long, almost endless days of the past year, today was flying by.

On the other hand, she'd slept almost four hours of daylight away, and that was a worry. Would she be able to sleep at bedtime? There were few things worse at night than insomnia, and she hated the idea that she'd just set herself up for a fresh bout of it.

After a brief shower and a head wash, she chose another pair of jeans and a shirt, managing a bra because she'd decided to drive to town. She didn't need anything in particular there, but the impulse to go was almost pleasant and she was desperate to hold onto the lighter feelings she'd had that day.

Margie scoffed when she came downstairs and announced she was driving to Coulter City.

"The last thing you need is the speed of highway driving," Margie warned. "Then there's the traffic in town."

"I'll be fine," Fay told her, "and I've got my cell phone."

"Cell phones are no good if you faint someplace."

"I don't faint," she declared, then started out the back door to head for the garage. Moments later, she was driving to the highway. It felt good to be leaving the ranch. Even her headache had improved, and she switched on the radio.

As she started to accelerate on the two-lane highway, a wisp of anticipation began to gently tease at her. Maybe she'd see what kind of storm damage Coulter City had gotten. It had been so long since she'd gone anywhere near a shopping mall that the idea was attractive. She might even eat supper in town, and made a mental note to phone Margie to let her know.

The novelty of wanting to go someplace and doing it provided an inkling of pleasure, but by the time she'd driven past some storm damage, meandered through the mall window-shopping and bought a taco in the food court, the pleasure had leaked away.

Though she'd gone to town and actually done a couple of things she hadn't done in ages, she'd done it all alone and that bothered her. It wasn't just that she missed having the boys along, but she suddenly missed her friends.

Unfortunately it was nearly 8:00 p.m., too late to drop by to say hello on a weeknight. And she'd avoided everyone so long that it wouldn't be simple to just walk in and take up where she'd left off. The last any of them had heard from her, she hadn't been up to socializing, so they'd eventually given up and gone on with their lives.

She regretted that now, and bleakness began to trickle back as she drove home. Until that moment she hadn't given a thought to facing another solitary homecoming to an empty house. If she had, she might not have taken the trip to town in the first place, and she certainly would have planned to get back while Margie was still there.

By the time she made her way up to bed she was achy and weary and felt so lonely she wanted to cry. Not for the first time she wished someone could wave a magic wand over her life and make everything like it used to be.

As she lay down on her bed and covered up, she began to wish for a way to get *herself* back to the way she used to be. The old Fay Sheridan would have known how to get on with her life and done it without a second thought. That Fay Sheridan had had heart and a will big enough and strong enough to do anything. The shadow that passed for Fay Sheridan these days couldn't seem to remember how to do anything important, much less find the energy to reconnect with what remained of her old life and the people she still had left.

The idea that she'd lost the knack to live increased the sense of loss she felt, and she stared up at the darkened ceiling lost in self-pity before she finally rolled over and went to sleep.

* * *

Fay pushed herself those next days, forcing her bruised body through normal chores and taking on work she should have avoided. The depression that dogged her every step made her short-tempered and easily frustrated. It also increased her carelessness, but despite Margie's objections and at least one remark from Riley that made her feel guilty, she soldiered on.

It was as if her few hours of feeling better the other day needed to be atoned for, as if her heart was compelled to exact a punishment, not only for taking a little enjoyment from life without her brothers, but also for wanting to live life as she used to. Logically she was aware that she shouldn't feel guilty, but emotionally it was easier not to fight the dark feelings. They just seemed too big and overwhelming.

The week ended and the weekend crawled past. Chase had said he'd stop by for her answer in a few days but he hadn't, and she realized she was just as angry with him for forgetting about her as she would have been if he'd shown up.

His proposal had continued to work on her when she hadn't been paying attention, tantalizing her with the idea of something new that might break the mind-numbing sameness of her days and nights.

She knew he hadn't been serious, but for once she might have welcomed another intrusion. Chase was the only person who'd dared to keep coming around, and though she scolded herself for needing some kind of conflict or shakeup in her life that wasn't life-threatening, her brain kept coming back to the idea of marrying him.

She could do a lot worse than marry Chase Rafferty. He was decent and hard-working, he cared about the things she used to care about and she'd fancied herself in love with him once. Though she didn't want to love him again, she almost liked him. He'd turned out to be good company the other night during the storms. And though she didn't care much about the sex part of marriage, she figured it might be possible to enjoy it on a physical level. From time to time.

The most important thing to her, aside from preserving Sheridan Ranch, was that Chase Rafferty would be a challenge she'd be forced to cope with, someone who would stick close enough to make her pay attention to someone outside of herself, someone to blast her out of the twilight life she led.

It was becoming more and more a shameful fact that she needed something novel to jolt her back to life and keep her there. Besides, if the old Fay ever did come back, she'd probably get a kick out of being married to the kind of husband Chase Rafferty would make.

Fay finally had to force herself to stop thinking about the "old" Fay and crazy ideas like marriage. She wasn't fit company for herself, much less anyone else, and the reminder made her deeply angry.

Chase knocked at the front door of the main house at Sheridan Ranch at midmorning on Monday. Seconds later, the door swung open, but instead of saying, "Hello," Miss Margie burst out with a worried, "Miss Fay's out workin' one of the green broke colts."

The disapproval and frustration on her face made it clear that Fay was on another reckless streak because she added, "She might still be down at the corrals, unless she's taken him to the range."

The front door swung closed with a snap, leaving Chase no doubt that Miss Margie expected him to do something.

Fay ought to be doing something for herself besides trying to get hurt. She probably thought she was doing something, since she'd become a workaholic, but the most she ever seemed to accomplish was to complicate things for the folks who cared about her. Even Riley had caught him in town and showed himself friendly, and though he hadn't said a thing about Fay, Chase had taken the hint that after the other night, both he and Miss Margie expected something from him.

It was more apparent to him now than ever that Fay was not just mad at life and what it had dealt her, but she had a fury going, as much toward herself as toward the way things had turned out. A good grief counselor could probably help untangle her from all that, but Fay wasn't someone who'd ask for that kind of help. She was too stubborn and too proud, oblivious to the idea that the same stubbornness and pride that had helped her survive this long was slowly killing her.

Chase went back to his pickup, mulling over the idea of marriage as he climbed in and drove out to the corrals. From the moment he realized he'd only been half kidding about suggesting marriage to Fay, he'd wavered between pushing for it and running like hell in the opposite direction. He was still a fraction more in favor of running when he spied the corral Fay was riding the colt in.

The woman was good to look at, whatever she was doing, and the pressure he felt to make up his mind eased. Just then, the colt threw his head down and gave a stiff-legged series of rodeo bucks that must have rattled Fay's teeth.

Chase braked to a stop and vaulted out of the truck as she stayed mounted, but he relaxed a little as she brought the sturdy bay back under control. The colt tried another couple of bucks before he calmed and walked along the fence rail as if he'd surrendered to the rider he'd failed to dislodge.

Fay's clothes were damp with sweat and her face was flushed. Going by the smudge of dirt down her right jeans' thigh and the elbow of her work shirt, she'd already taken at least one good spill. He'd bet she'd hurt every healing muscle in her body and strained a few more, and he could tell by the tightness of her lips that her head hurt.

Chase lifted his arms to rest them on the top rail of the corral to watch in a pose of unconcern. The woman had an uncommon measure of grit and he wondered how long it would be before she stopped using it to punish herself.

Another two circuits around the pen went smoothly so Fay pulled the colt to a halt next to the gate to dismount. As she did, her left knee buckled a little before she could catch herself, and he heard a soft swear word hiss from between her clenched teeth. The rough ride had set her back, and she should have known better. Yes, it had been a good six days since the storms, but she would have been facing some strained muscles from that ride even if she hadn't been hurt a few days before. And of course, she covered the hurt with grouchiness.

"D'ja get your buildings up?" she called out. It was a conversational thing to ask, but her grumpy tone spoiled it. "Thanks for fixing the fence," she added, as if she realized how cranky she'd sounded, though her tone didn't change much.

"The buildings are going up now. I see you're still aboveground," he nettled and she threw him a sharp look. "Hope you don't mind that I gave you a little extra time to think things over. What did you decide?"

The sharp look faltered and he realized he'd caught her off guard, but she recovered. "Make an offer. If I like the numbers, we'll write something up."

He shook his head. "This isn't about the lease."

She stared at him a moment, searching his face before her lashes dropped down and she turned away to reach for the gate latch. As she passed behind him, Chase glanced back and saw the grim set of her profile beneath her hat brim. He couldn't tell how much more he'd riled her, or if he had, but he certainly hadn't made her happy.

And that was fine with him. He wasn't sure he was happy about proposing marriage, but he couldn't quite bring himself to hope she'd refuse. It was past time for him to marry and settle down, and though he couldn't make a worse choice than Fay Sheridan in her present state, the idea of marrying her suddenly sent a prickly anticipation through him that countered more than a few misgivings.

The concern he'd felt for her after her brothers had been killed had deepened, and he realized he felt a connection to her that wouldn't be easy to break.

Plus, he remembered the way she used to be. She might never be quite the same again, but she'd had all the right stuff back then. She still did, despite her battle with grief and her trouble getting on with life. Things would eventually come right for Fay, and he wouldn't mind having a front row seat when they did.

He caught up and fell into step beside her. "How 'bout I call the airlines, see if we can get a flight to Las Vegas this afternoon? We could spend the rest of the week there after we tie the knot, catch some of the shows, gamble a little."

"I don't gamble," she said sourly, and he chuckled.

"You're a gambler all right, just not with money."

Chase's on-target assessment stung. Fay's temper flashed up. "What do you get out of it?"

"A wife. Kids eventually."

"What if I don't want kids? What if I don't feel like being a wife?"

"Have a little faith, Miss Fay," he drawled, and Fay felt her face go hot.

"You're pretty sure of yourself," she scoffed, and he came right back with, "Sometimes."

Fay handed off the colt to her wrangler and walked on. Chase kept up with her, but his longer legs took the distance at a more relaxed pace. Fay was wound tight and her stomach was doing flips. She was painfully excited, nervous and angry. Those feelings intensified when he persisted.

"So how 'bout it?"

"You'd be in a sorry state if I said yes," she groused, strangely unable to flat-out refuse.

"Maybe."

Fay glanced his way again, caught the glitter in his gaze and faced forward, increasing her pace. Her brain was suddenly like a pan of scrambled eggs, and her heart was pounding so hard and so fast that she could hear it thumping in her ears.

She'd call his bluff. Not for anything did she want Chase to know how much his offhand proposal had tormented—and maybe tantalized—her. It was a joke; it couldn't be anything else, despite his pretense now. She could put a quick end to it if she said yes. He'd either have to put up or shut up, and she was certain he'd choose to shut up.

Suddenly *very* certain of that, Fay came to a halt at the edge of the patio and turned to him. "All right. Let's do it now. We'll call the airlines on the way to San Antonio, fly to Vegas, get it done then get on a plane and be home by tonight."

"No honeymoon?"

"We don't need the trimmings. This is business, right?"

He didn't answer that, and she was too agitated to notice as he glanced down the front of her.

"Don't you want to get cleaned up, change your clothes?" he asked, his mouth going into a faint smirk. "Maybe put on a dress?"

His continued perusal felt remarkably personal.

"So you're getting cold feet already."

He shook his head. "Just thinking how uncomfortable it'll be to travel in sweaty clothes."

"All right," she said, suddenly determined to run him off. "Meet me back here in an hour."

His gaze zoomed up to fasten on hers. "Then your answer is yes." His gaze probed hers for several seconds.

Fay shrugged. "Sure, why not? Just remember, this was your bright idea."

With that she turned away and walked on into the house, leaving Chase to do whatever he was going to do. She didn't think for a moment he'd actually come back in an hour to take her to Vegas. He'd been so quiet there at the end, watching her closely as if he was wondering how serious she was.

Let him wonder. This whole marriage idea was beginning to hurt. There'd been a time when she would have loved to have Chase Rafferty ask her to marry him, but now that the last thing she wanted was to love somebody who could die an early death, he'd made a joke of asking her.

Even worse, he'd made her *think* about marrying him, over and over and obsessively. And of course her dying heart had grabbed onto the idea like a lifeline. She was more than a little ashamed of that.

She should have told him no right away. *Should* have. She still could, but she couldn't seem to do it, even now. Besides, it would look like she was taking this seriously and she'd hate for him to think that, whether it was true or not.

Fay stalked into the house and stopped at the refrigerator intending to get out the iced tea pitcher. *She should call Chase's cell phone and tell him to forget about coming back—ever.* Stop this idiotic game, whatever it was.

Miss Margie bustled into the kitchen as she stared at the refrigerator door, about to lapse into what Miss Margie sometimes called "the ninety-minute stare." The housekeeper derailed the possibility when she nudged Fay aside and got out the pitcher.

"I see you're still in one piece," the woman remarked as she got a tall glass out of the cupboard and poured the tea before she handed it to Fay. "Looks like that colt wrung you out and rolled you in the dust."

Fay took the glass with a quick thanks, and drank half of it down before she held it out for Margie to refill. "Chase Rafferty's coming back in an hour to take me to Vegas."

Margie almost dropped the pitcher and took in a long, disbelieving gasp. "So you said yes!"

"I'm pulling his leg," Fay said with a shake of her head. "He's not serious. I doubt we'll see him for at least a month. Good riddance."

Margie set the pitcher aside. "He wouldn't tease about something like that, would he?"

"Well, he can't want to marry me," Fay pointed out as she lifted the glass. She took another long drink of the refill before the chill of the cold liquid made her pause. Margie was staring at her as if she was about to settle into some serious grilling, so that was her cue to leave.

"I need to get cleaned up," Fay said, then downed the rest of her iced tea and set the empty glass on the counter before she crossed the kitchen to the back stairs.

Forty-five minutes later, Fay was clean and in fresh jeans and a T-shirt. As she did bookwork at the computer and nibbled a few corn chips from a bowl, she tried not to watch the clock. She'd already turned on the small TV in the den to provide background noise so she wouldn't be listening for the sound of Chase's pickup or his car.

Though she was fairly certain he wouldn't show up, her nerves weren't so convinced. Ten minutes later—*fifty-five minutes* since she'd walked away from Chase in the yard—Margie came rushing into the room, her face bright with excitement and wearing the widest smile Fay had seen in a year. She snapped off the TV with an expert smack of her fingers on the switch.

"He's here!" Margie declared in a confidential hiss, as if she was afraid Chase might overhear. "And you thought he wasn't serious! Oh, I wish you had a white dress!"

Fay couldn't move for those next seconds. Chase was here? As if she'd asked the question aloud, Margie babbled on, coming around the desk to pull her out of her chair.

"He's wearing a gorgeous pin-striped suit and a black dress Stetson. He makes such a handsome groom!"

Fay let herself be pulled to her feet, not only shocked that Chase was actually here, but shocked at how charged up Margie was. She tried to calm the woman. "Even if he's serious, Margie, surely you don't approve?"

Margie barely thought about it. "I'd rather things were different, but Mr. Rafferty's the biggest catch in this part of

Texas. And he cares about you, Fay. Any fool can see that. Maybe he—"

She cut herself off briefly and amended whatever she'd been about to say to, "He might be the biggest catch in this part of Texas among the men, but for my money, you're the biggest female catch. Yes, you've had your troubles, but those don't make you any less attractive, not to a man who knows your heart."

The insanity of the moment finally struck Fay, and a bubble of hilarity gurgled out. "Knows my *heart?*" She giggled again. "Margie, listen to yourself."

"I know all about what I sound like, Fay, and I'm telling you to get upstairs so I can open the door for Mr. Chase. If he's got a plane lined up, you don't want to be late." Margie practically dragged her around the desk then through the doorway into the hall.

Impatient with Fay's lack of enthusiasm, she let go of her arm and gave her a push toward the kitchen to hurry her along, then bustled toward the front hall when Fay complied.

Fay did go up the back stairs, at first so she could peek down the front staircase to see for herself how Chase was dressed and how he seemed. The moment she caught sight of the formal suit and the way he pulled off his dress Stetson as he walked inside, she saw the somberness about him and her heart nearly leaped out of her chest.

There was no mistaking the no-nonsense grimness about him; she doubted he was a good enough actor to fake that. Especially when Margie fluttered around him like a little bird, cautiously questioning him, and nodding emphatically at his one-word answers.

Though Fay couldn't hear what Margie was asking, the woman seemed more than pleased with his answers so Fay slipped into her bedroom, closed the door and leaned back against it as she grappled with the idea that Chase really did mean to marry her.

But thinking about it and doing it were worlds away from each other. Could she really go through with this? Did she really want to? She'd called his bluff, but now he'd called hers, so it was time to up the ante or fold.

That's when she heard Margie coming up the front stairs.

CHAPTER FIVE

THAT evening, Mr. and Mrs. Chase Rafferty got off the return flight from Las Vegas to start the drive back to Coulter City. Neither of them spoke, which didn't appear to trouble Mr. Rafferty. Mrs. Rafferty was troubled by things that had nothing to do with the lack of conversation.

She'd married Chase! She'd gone with him to Las Vegas, taken a cab to a wedding chapel, answered in all the right places as they were led through the traditional vows, then stared stupidly as he'd slipped an antique gold band on her finger. She'd stood there just as stupidly looking up at him as he'd leaned down to give her a quick cool kiss after they'd been pronounced husband and wife. Her lips had burned ever since.

Chase seemed relaxed as he drove the long ribbon of dark highway, and though he was silent he appeared to be enjoying himself. He'd been like that long before they'd boarded their flight to San Antonio, and it annoyed her. Now there was a strong hint of satisfaction about him, as if he had everything he wanted and was content with the world.

You'd be in a sorry state if you married me, she'd warned him that morning. She'd been such a witch this past year that she'd assumed she'd continue to be as cranky and out of sorts with him as she usually was.

But she was the one in the sorry state. She'd been completely cowed by the vows they'd spoken, taking them far more seriously than she'd ever imagined she would and in the end she'd felt the weight of them in a way that subdued the idea of making anyone's life miserable, much less Chase's.

She'd figured marrying him would shake things up and she'd be forced to cope with something besides grief, but she was a nervous wreck over it all. She'd gone through every emotion that day except a panic attack, and she wasn't too sure she wouldn't yet have one.

Too soon the car slowed, and Fay realized they were about to turn onto the Rafferty/Keenan Ranch road. The drive from San Antonio had never seemed so fast! Her stomach knotted tight as the car left the highway and began to accelerate on the long graveled driveway. She'd be staying at Chase's place tonight. Though she'd tried to think of some way to avoid sharing a bed with him, every excuse she'd thought of shouted cowardice. Pride demanded she behave as if she didn't care where either of them slept, but all she could think about was to wonder how on earth she'd be able to stand being that close to him.

Yes, they'd spent the night at her house a week ago, but there'd been nothing to that. The idea of sharing a bed was a major step toward intimacy and a traditional wedding night.

The only thing that gave her comfort was to remember that this wasn't a love match for either of them. They'd only jumped into this so suddenly because she'd been in a bad mood and called Chase's bluff. And it wasn't as if he had lustful designs on her body. Except for that kiss today and a little tepid handholding, Chase had been the soul of propriety. Hardly an amorous groom eager to seduce his bride.

It was even possible they wouldn't sleep together tonight. The main house at the

R/K had guest rooms, so he might be planning to give her one of those. If not, then Chase would choose his side of the bed, she'd choose hers, and the most significant thing that would happen would be that she'd find out if he snored.

A few of her nerves unknotted at the idea and Fay began to relax. It had been a long day and she was tired enough to fall asleep the moment her head hit the pillow. Chase probably felt the same way.

Chase slowed the car again and turned off the ranch road onto the pavement that curved in front of the house. Only a few lights were on in the main part of the sprawling single-story home, but the warm glow was welcoming and oddly reassuring.

Fay had always liked Chase's house. With everything on one level, there were no stairs to climb at the end of a weary day, and practically every room on the back of the house opened onto a richly landscaped patio. Because she loved the outdoors, the idea of being able to step into the outside air anytime, even from her bedroom, was appealing.

The sound of the car engine switching off made her glance Chase's way, but he already had his car door open and was getting out. Not one to stand on ceremony, she opened her own door and got out just as he came around the hood of the car.

He'd shed his suit jacket and tie, and though he'd folded back the cuffs of his dress shirt, he still looked as fresh as he had at the ceremony. It was the new ease about him that got her attention and signaled his pleasure at returning home. The fact that he suddenly looked more handsome than she'd ever seen him wasn't exactly a comfort, especially not when she felt a deep flutter of attraction.

She turned away intending to walk to the

back of the car to get her luggage from the trunk, but Chase caught her hand.

"Someone else'll bring in your things," he said and just as easily picked her up to stride to the front door.

The surprise of being swept up to be carried over the threshold like a genuine bride set off little alarms.

"I thought we were skipping these parts," she babbled out. "None of the trimmings, right?"

"A little tradition here and there won't hurt," he said. "Aren't these little things meant for good luck?"

"I don't know—"

"I thought you women knew all about wedding folderol. Didn't you have any ambition in the way of marriage?"

Fay wasn't about to answer that and didn't need to because Chase stopped at the front door. He leaned down enough to turn the doorknob before he straightened and nudged the door open with the toe of his boot. He walked over the threshold, paused to kick the door shut then walked into the middle of the large foyer and stopped.

He slowly lowered her feet to the floor, but it seemed he held her the slightest bit too close when he did. The moment her shoes touched the solid tile, she started to back up. Chase caught her waist before she could and his fingers flexed gently to keep her little more than an inch away. Her hands had no place to go but to his shirtfront, and the hardness and heat that scorched her palms made her sharply aware of him as a man. The thump of his heart beneath her fingers was forceful and emphasized the drumbeat of life in his veins.

The raw masculinity of the man, despite his civilized, city clothes, made a deep impression on her and a feeling of weakness swept through her that shocked her to her toes. His natural dominance made an equally deep impression and was underscored by the glittering intent in his darkening eyes as he leaned down and his mouth fastened firmly on hers.

Taken by surprise, Fay started to turn her face away, but the forceful kiss turned gentle and the tender expertise of his firm lips made it impossible to move. The contact deepened so fast it made her head spin and she felt herself go weaker. Thank heavens the kiss didn't last long, but when Chase drew back he appeared completely unaffected. Meanwhile, she was clinging to his shirtfront, her knees almost too unsteady to support her. And her lips were burning again, though this time the burn had scorched her insides, too.

His low, "Welcome home, Mrs. Rafferty," mocked her earlier ideas of what kind of business their business marriage was about. If she didn't know better, she'd almost think…

"I suppose we ought to do the grand tour so you'll know where everything is," he was saying, more practical—and still obviously unaffected—than she was yet capable of being. Didn't anything rattle this man? "Then we'll have a late supper."

Chase released her waist to take her hand and lead the way through the main rooms at the center of the big house. Truth to tell, she'd needed him to lead her around and somehow distract her from what had just happened. The problem was that having her hand smothered and warmed by the callused strength of his kept the piercingly sensual feelings from the kiss echoing through her. She finally managed to pull her hand from his and get some shred of normalcy back.

The living room was furnished with heavy leather furniture and dark wood tables that were brightened by the strong colors of woven rugs, oil paintings and plump throw pillows, some of them embroidered and aged. The floor beneath it all was a golden oak with a mellow shine whose rich color harmonized with the lighter gold of the walls. The overall effect was a blend of drama and the kind of comfort that was unique enough to qualify for a decorating magazine. It was a style that was echoed through the rest of the house, especially the den.

The kitchen, which had food cooking, was large with lots of pristine white tile and rich color, and opened to a comfy family room on one side and a swinging door on the other that led to the formal dining room. The den was located on the far side of the family room and not only had an entrance from there, but also a door from the inner hall of the house and a wide set of double glass doors to the patio.

As she'd remembered, all the rooms along the back of the house opened onto the patio, which looked more like a private garden with shade trees and flowers bordered by tall trellises and flowering vines.

The color and vitality of it all dazzled her, and Fay realized with a pang how somber and lifeless her home seemed by comparison. The pang changed quickly to a feeling of guilt that made her homesick.

Even without that staggering kiss in the foyer, once Chase showed her through the guest wing of the big house, she realized her chances of being offered one of those rooms were nil. Any of them were too far from the family wing of the house and would therefore make it too noticeable if they slept apart.

Chase's unspoken pride of family and home was very clear to her now. Too clear to miss the idea that pride would also dictate appearances. A man as macho as

Chase might enter into a loveless marriage of convenience, but she doubted very much he'd tolerate separate bedrooms, much less separate lives. Which made her worry even more about that kiss.

They finally reached the master suite at the very end of the family wing, and Fay became dismally certain of what was ahead in the next months and years of married life. The suite included its own sitting area and boasted a common walk-in closet with a huge bath to fully accommodate a husband and wife. From the double sinks to the roomy shower and huge bathtub with room for two, it was all just right for a couple and indicated an expectation of togetherness and intimacy.

Any idea of having a truly long-lasting nontraditional arrangement based solely on business with nothing more complicated between them deflated even more. Well, she'd asked for this, though she couldn't seem to fully remember why beyond an idea of ensuring the future of Sheridan Ranch and the fact that she'd been in a foul mood that morning. That all seemed so, so minor now, and certainly not worth the new hazards that suddenly loomed large. Hazards like becoming a genuine part of Chase Rafferty's life and him becoming a genuine part of hers…

"We'd better get out to supper," Chase said, his quiet suggestion exploding on touchy nerves and making her jump a little. He ushered her out of the bathroom and through the sitting area of the suite to the patio doors.

They stepped outside to a small table spread with a white tablecloth and Fay's heart fell. A vase of red roses sat to the side, next to a candelabra that had already been lit. Two place settings of fine china with covers sat across from each other and a small white cake with a tiny bride and groom sat on a pedestal plate that was covered by a tall glass lid. A bucket of ice that held a bottle of champagne sat next to the roses and once Chase seated her, he pulled the bottle out of the ice and efficiently opened it.

Whoever was responsible for the elegantly romantic little setting and hot food was nowhere in sight and Fay watched, dazed by the ongoing avalanche of the unexpected—and unwanted—as Chase poured the wine and sat down. He lifted his wine flute, which prompted her to reach for hers and follow suit, though her hand visibly trembled. Chase didn't appear to notice.

"To a new beginning together," he said then touched her glass with his before they drank to it. "If you have something to add, now's a good time."

Fay couldn't have come up with a toast to save her neck. What could she say anyway? *Here's hoping I can move back home—tomorrow, if not tonight?*

"You...took care of it pretty well," she got out, unable to keep the glumness completely out of her voice. She quickly downed her champagne, hoping that ended talk of other toasts. Taking the alcohol so fast made her cough a little.

As if he didn't notice that, either, Chase briskly refilled her wine flute then lifted the covers off their plates, revealing steamed vegetables and beef medallions in a dark sauce. Fay thought she'd be too nervous to eat much, but the food was delicious and she finished it all.

"Whoever cooked this did a wonderful job," she felt obliged to say, though she omitted a compliment on the romantic setting.

"This is Miss Ilsa's doing. And just so you'll know, she thinks we need to have a reception of some kind. It wouldn't surprise me if she's already made a call to your Miss Margie about it."

The news gave her a queasy feeling. The last thing she wanted was the fuss and bother—and especially the attention—a wedding reception would bring. People would naturally be expecting that this was a normal marriage with a lot of lovey-dovey romantic behavior between the bride and groom. If they didn't see it, there would be questions and a lot more gossip and speculation than there'd be over two people who'd simply eloped.

Chase's low voice interrupted her thoughts.

"So you're not thrilled with the idea of a reception." Her gaze shot to his to gauge how he was taking that. His half smile indicated he was amused.

"We don't exactly have the kind of arrangement that'll pass muster with a lot of the people we know," she pointed out, glad to have some way to remind him that this marriage was about business, not about doing more of what had happened in the foyer. "How many business marriages are there around here?"

"Not many," he allowed. "I think a reception's a good idea. Let folks know you're ready to be sociable again, but with the added idea that you've got a husband, so your free time isn't completely your own. That way, you can choose how sociable you want to be and no one will think a thing of it."

What he said made sense, but she shook her head. "It isn't just about being sociable. People have expectations of newlyweds, how they behave with each oth—"

Fay cut herself off, appalled she'd put it that way. It almost sounded as if she was hinting that they become *true* newlyweds. Her face went hot as one corner of Chase's mouth curled a little deeper and he leaned back in his chair as if she'd blundered into a tantalizing subject.

"So it worries you to think that all they'll see between us are lease agreements and dollar signs." He was enjoying this and she felt a spurt of temper.

"Fine. Have your wedding reception," she grumbled to close the subject, and finished off the last of her champagne. It was actually her third glass, but it wasn't mellowing her mood much.

"So that kiss a while ago makes you optimistic after all," he said. "Me, too. No tellin' what sort of things folk'll see between us in another day or two."

Fay's face heated even more as panic and frustration went through her, followed closely by a confusing flare of longing that was as unwelcome as it was unexpected. What was wrong with her? Was it the alcohol?

Chase was playing with her, he had to be. That kiss hadn't affected him at all, yet he seemed to know precisely how it had affected her. She didn't have enough experience with men to have been able to control her reaction, and that probably amused a man of the world like him. He was teasing her about it now because he was in annoyingly good spirits, she was the only one around to focus them on, and they didn't have a lot to do except make conversation.

"You're way too full of yourself, cowboy. Who's going to clear the table?" The quicker she could change the subject away from receptions and newlyweds and kisses, the better.

"Miss Ilsa. In the morning. Should we sample the cake now or have it with breakfast?"

Fay set her napkin beside her plate but said, "That's up to you." Chase set his own napkin on the table and stood.

"If you want to take in the flowers and our glasses, I'll put out the candles and bring the champagne."

Relieved Chase was done teasing, Fay stood and reached for the vase of roses, snagged each of their wine flutes and carried them into the bedroom. She set the flutes and the vase on the low table in the sitting area of the master suite and couldn't resist touching a velvety red bloom or two as Chase came in, easily managing the ice bucket and champagne in the crook of his arm while he carried the pedestal plate with the cake and bell cover.

She could hardly expect him to leave the cake outside, even if it did have a secure cover, but seeing the little bride and groom standing so earnestly together on top in the lamplight suddenly made her emotional. Maybe the champagne *was* affecting her.

Chase set the ice bucket next to the

roses, then the pedestal plate before he straightened and reached back to pull the napkin-wrapped cake knife from his back pocket. The boyish stunt almost startled a laugh out of her and Fay suddenly felt guilty for being such a killjoy.

"We ought to at least have a couple bites of this before we turn in," he said.

Fay made herself sit in one of the overstuffed chairs next to the table to humor him as he lifted off the glass dome of the cake plate to efficiently cut a wedge of the fluffy confection. He used the flat of the cake knife to lift the slice and lay it on its side on a napkin.

"I think the groom offers his bride the first bite," he said, then hunkered down in front of her chair to hold the napkin and cake toward her. "At least this one will."

Wary, Fay tried to be as casual about it as possible as she leaned toward him to take the expected bite before she drew back.

The cake tasted wonderful, but it instantly turned to sawdust in her mouth when Chase said, “Your turn.”

Fay took the napkin and offered Chase the second bite. Because her hand trembled, Chase reached up to encircle her wrist with his fingers and took a big bite of cake.

His low, “Mmm,” set off a flutter in her middle as he savored the frosted bite. He released her wrist and took over the napkin again. “Have some more,” he coaxed, and she made herself take another bite before Chase reached up to pluck the last of the slim cake wedge off the napkin to finish it.

Glad to be done with the little ritual, Fay set the napkin aside but Chase’s gaze zeroed in on her mouth. Figuring she had a stray bit of cake frosting where it didn’t belong, she quickly reached up to brush the corner of her mouth. Chase caught her hand and leaned close enough to lick the bit of frosting off her finger.

A warm sensation flashed through her and impacted low, stirring up the weakness he'd inflicted on her earlier and bringing with it fresh echoes of what she now recognized as desire. The satisfied gleam in Chase's eyes preceded a swiftly gathering intensity that was pure male intent. Her mouth went dry.

"I don't know about you," he drawled, "but I'm ready to make it a night."

Fay stood so suddenly that Chase fell back a little, then unbent his knees to stand to his full six-foot-plus height. That alone reasserted his male dominance and she abruptly turned away to make her escape. Once her back was turned, Chase caught her waist to stop her.

"Let me take care of that zipper," he said and before she could refuse, he had the thing partway down her back. And of course that set off a fresh rash of tingles when the zipper caught on the top of her slip and he had to reach up with his other hand to help free it. The back of his fingers grazed her skin and sent a tremor through her that was part female excitement and part pure fear.

"If I didn't say so before," he murmured, his warm breath on her upper back sending a new flood of weakness through her, "I like this little blue dress you picked for today. Makes your eyes go lighter. Shows off your…everything."

The lazy way he said that wrapped her in an invisible web of sensuality that made her slow to realize that his warm fingertips were stroking her shoulders and that the neckline of the dress had slipped to her upper arms. Those same warm fingertips began to toy with her slip straps.

Never had her inexperience with men seemed so stark. She was actually falling under the spell of Chase's sexy drawl and knowledgeable touch. It amazed her to find out she was so susceptible to so little.

There was still time to stop this. She sensed she could step away from him at any time and he'd accept it, but the realization was dangerous. Dangerous because her body didn't feel like moving away just yet, and she began to give in to the temptation to delay. Something deep inside her was starved for the sensual contact he was slowly introducing. The year of grief and isolation she'd endured had made her needy, too needy to obey what remained of her common sense or natural caution.

The craving to be close to someone, to be close to *Chase,* was so primitive and overwhelming that she began to tremble with the effort it took not to turn to him for more. If she didn't get away from him that moment, she'd be lost, stampeded toward someone and into something her heart couldn't bear to face.

Precious seconds ebbed past quickly and just as quickly pulled at the crumbling self-will she'd always thought was so formidable. The hot brush of Chase's firm lips on the top of her shoulder made her senses leap high enough to erode a little more of her will. When those lips nibbled to her neck, her head eased to the side in half-realized permission and grant of access.

She'd been so lonely, so desperately heartbroken, filled with the kind of pride that had goaded her to weather it all alone. To her great harm.

When Chase's strong arms slid around her from behind and slowly pulled her back against his wonderful heat, she felt the comfort of his closeness and it suddenly didn't matter that there was no love in any of this. Something devastated and lonely inside her was feeling the first promise of relief and in a few moments more the last scrap of pride that might have helped her put a stop to this fell away.

The craving to be soothed and the deep need to survive long enough to truly grasp life again, made her incapable of resisting.

CHAPTER SIX

THE sense of peace and well-being was so profound that they must have been the lingering effects of a powerful dream, and Fay snuggled deeper into the bed, sleepily enjoying the warmth that wrapped around her so snugly as she mentally searched for remnants of the dream.

Instead of finding them, reality began to reclaim her, pulling her toward the dreaded start of another long, wearying day. In the next second, she identified the source of the uncommon warmth that cocooned her, and came fully and brutally awake.

Her eyes popped open to see that the bedside lamps were still on, and memories of the night before tumbled through her brain like colored chips in a kaleidoscope, arranging and rearranging bits and snatches of sights and sensations that sent fire over her skin from scalp to toes.

Fay abruptly bolted from the bed, throwing off a heavy arm and tangled covers then freezing two steps from the bed as she realized she was stark naked. A male chuckle from the bed behind her ignited a fireball of mortification.

Chase's lazy greeting was low and rusty. "'Mornin', Miss Fay."

Fay jerked her arms up to fold them over her breasts and turn partway toward the bed in a futile effort to cover herself and to remove the full on backside view Chase was getting. She felt the satin coolness of her discarded slip under her foot and dipped down gratefully to snatch it up. She sorted it out and dragged it over her head to yank it down so she was decently covered. By then Chase had risen to lean on one elbow and look on. He shook his head.

"That slip's not worth the effort, darlin'. I've got too good a memory."

Fay was practically vibrating with anger and the sexy smirk he was giving her made things worse. "Good for you. It'll give you something to remember over the next sixty years."

Chase feigned a disgruntled look. "Sixty?"

"At least!" she hissed before she turned and stalked to the bathroom, slamming the door hard enough to rattle a picture frame on the wall.

Chase fell back against his pillow, unable to stop the smile that stretched wide. He lay there a moment before he threw the covers off and got up to stroll to the closet and choose a set of clothes. He just had time to notice that the closet door into the bathroom was still open a crack before it too slammed shut.

If Fay hadn't been so cranky, he might have opened that door and gone in to join her in the shower, but they had years ahead of them for that. Right now it was better to let her cool off. Meanwhile, he'd shower in one of the other bathrooms.

As he walked out into the bedroom and opened the door to cross the hall, Chase realized he felt a contentment that was new to him. He'd made Fay his last night, and in spite of her ire that morning, she'd managed in her own way to make him hers.

She'd been a virgin, and if that hadn't been special enough, sex with her had been different. He wasn't one to use words like "profound," but that was the only word that described it. Marriage was a very good thing.

Though it seemed he might be the only one who looked forward to the next time, he felt the optimism of the very vivid memory he'd mentioned to Fay. There'd been no mistaking her response to him: at first hesitant, then shy, and before long, welcoming and generously expressive. She'd been so soft and pliant afterward, as if she was just as happy and satisfied as he'd been. She'd melted against him in those minutes after the stars had cartwheeled, exchanging slow and weary kisses and touches, as if they'd meant something as sweet to her as they had to him.

She wasn't the kind of woman who'd take any of that lightly, but she *was* the kind of woman who'd recover her pride by morning and throw a couple bricks in his direction to hold him off so she could reerect a wall.

But it didn't matter. Neither of them could take back last night. Because she'd been raised to take marriage as seriously as he did, she'd eventually make peace with what they'd done. And with what *she'd* done. Her loss of control last night was likely the cause of her prickliness just now. She probably hadn't realized it was possible.

Chase grinned at that, torn between amusement and a touch of masculine pride as he twisted on the shower faucet and adjusted the temperature.

Fay stepped out of the shower, vigorously rubbed herself dry with one towel and squeezed the excess wetness from her hair with another. When she peeked into the walk-in closet, the door to the bedroom was closed and she rushed out, hurriedly ripping underwear and a cotton shirt and jeans from one of her suitcases before she dressed. Another peek from the closet into the bedroom showed her that Chase was nowhere to be seen, so she stalked out to round up her clothes.

Roundup was the right word for the search. Her dress had been tossed to a bedside chair, but her bra and panty hose were scattered on the floor around the big bed. Except for her panties. Those she found tangled in the sheets at the foot of the bed.

That's when her temper leaked away. She hadn't been forced to participate in a thing last night, and the truth was there hadn't been that much seduction. She'd knowingly and willingly allowed what had happened. Even worse, she'd wanted it. They were husband and wife. In spite of her fixation on a marriage based on business, the vows they'd taken yesterday had opened a mental door that had made last night inevitable.

Fay sat down on the edge of the mattress, defeated. If she'd had any doubts before about her judgment, she had plenty of doubts now. She'd made a royal mess of her life, on purpose. How could it not have been on purpose? She'd seen marriage to Chase as a way to shake up her life. Well, her life had truly been shaken, and she'd agreed to allow it at every step. Directing her anger toward Chase instead of herself was the coward's way.

Chastened, she rose and carried her things to the closet and shut them in one of her suitcases. The urge to run away from what she'd done was so strong suddenly she could taste it, but pride demanded she stay and face the consequences.

Thank God the consequences wouldn't include pregnancy, because it was the wrong time of her cycle. She'd known that yesterday, but she needed to call her doctor the moment she could and make an emergency appointment for birth control.

She walked out into the bedroom, reluctant to face her new husband. Memories of the night before still sent heat to her face, and now the tangled bedclothes on the bed reminded her of how uninhibited she'd been. Embarrassed to have Ilsa see that, she hurried to the bedside and switched off one of the lamps before she straightened the top sheet and pulled it toward the pillows. She dragged the comforter up and smoothed it into place before she hurried to the other side. She was just finishing when Chase walked in from the hall.

"Still mad at me?"

She heard the smile in his voice and glanced his way. Dressed in a green shirt and newer jeans, clean-shaven, his dark hair still damp from his shower, Chase looked handsome and fresh and so appealing that Fay felt her chest tighten with something unexpectedly emotional. Regret was all but strangling her and she was compelled to do something about it.

"I was out of line earlier," she said, hoping to get this over with. "I apologize." She made herself look him directly in the eye as he walked over to her. There was no hint of triumph in his gaze, only a kindness that shamed her even more.

"Maybe not too far out of line," he allowed as he settled his big hands on her waist. "I seduced you, Fay. And I meant to."

"Why?" The word was out of her mouth before common sense could stop her.

"A man takes a wife, and some powerful instincts get stirred. Plus, it's better to start as we mean to go." A slow, sexy smile angled across his handsome mouth. "Then there was that blue dress."

Heat scorched her cheeks and her gaze fled his. It shocked her a little to realize that a silly little smile was trying to break free and it flustered her. But not enough to overlook what he'd said just before his remark about her dress. She gave him a narrow look. "What do you mean, 'Start as we mean to go'?"

"I mean exactly that. This is a marriage, and sex is part of it."

Fay felt her cheeks heat again and stepped back from him a little. She sensed if she challenged him on the subject that he could easily point out that she'd not been unwilling. Another flash of memory underscored that. She'd not only been—or become—willing, she'd been…eager.

"Nothing more to say about last night?" he prompted and she shook her head. She was just about to turn to walk out of the room toward the kitchen and breakfast when he caught her hand and leaned down to kiss her.

Her mouth automatically molded itself to his as if kissing him was as normal for her as breathing, and if that wasn't bad enough, she felt herself sway closer. His hand came up and fastened firmly on the back of her neck and he deepened the kiss as he drew her against himself.

She was suddenly awash in the piercing hungers he'd brought her to last night. Without conscious thought, her hands slid up his chest to wind around his neck. The kiss was a morning replay of one of the hottest ones they'd shared. It reduced Fay to the trembling, weak-kneed novice she'd been last night and she was soon clinging to him. When Chase pulled his lips away and crushed her tighter against himself, she snuggled her cheek against the side of his neck, unable to keep from holding on to him just as tightly.

Her body was all but throbbing with the heady pulse of desire and she almost moaned when Chase loosened his arms and drew back to lead her to the hall with one arm around her shoulders. How her weak knees supported her was a mystery and she needed the support of the arm she'd slid around his lean waist. She was in deep, deep trouble.

“Might be too late to have breakfast on the patio,” Chase was saying, as if he hadn’t noticed her reaction or sensed her distress over it, “but we’ll see where Miss Ilsa’s set our plates.”

The mention of his housekeeper made Fay strive harder to regain her equilibrium. She sneaked a touch to her lips and realized she probably looked like she’d had the daylights kissed out of her. Just before they reached the dining room door, she managed to let go of Chase’s waist and pull away enough to make sure her hair wasn’t mussed.

And of course that’s when she realized she hadn’t dried it and she made a mad effort to finger-comb it into place. Miss Ilsa was waiting as they walked in and Fay tried to give a normal-looking smile.

There were fresh flowers decorating the long formal table. This bouquet was a plethora of colorful blooms placed next to two place settings of fine china and elegant glassware that had been carefully set out.

Fay murmured the appropriate words as she was introduced to Ilsa, then felt compelled to compliment her not only on the beautiful table setting this morning, but on the romantic setting last night.

"You went to a lot of trouble," she added and Miss Ilsa beamed, her lively expression and sparkling brown eyes communicating her pleasure at the compliments.

"It'll be nice to get out the fancy things around here, things you can't put on a bachelor's table. Welcome to the R/K. I hope you'll be happy here and raise lots of little Raffertys."

Fay kept her smile and said a quiet thanks before Ilsa rushed out to start their breakfast. Chase was on hand to pull out her chair for her and seated himself once she sat down.

"How much business do you have to do this week?" he asked and Fay relaxed.

Now they were in safe territory and she meant to make the most of it.

"There's never any end to the work, you know that. I'd like to get back to it right after breakfast." What she wanted more than anything was time alone so she could recover from what they'd done.

"I thought it might be nice to ease up on business for a few days," he persisted. "How long's it been since you spent a day just being lazy?"

"A while." In fact, it had been a year. The idea of lazing around doing nothing worthwhile made her uneasy. Chase spoke as if he'd read her mind on the subject.

"If you can't handle it, we'll find something to do," he said as Ilsa carried in a tray of food. "But we ought to get to Coulter City and take care of a thing or two."

Ilsa began with a carafe of coffee that she poured and set aside. She then set a serving of the thick, meaty quiche she'd brought on each of their plates and placed a bowl of sliced fruit and melon between them that was topped by a big dollop of whipped cream. When she'd finished and they'd thanked her, Ilsa took the tray and left the room.

Determined to reassert whatever space between the two of them that she could, Fay said, "I can't think of a thing I need to do in town today."

Chase passed her the bowl of fruit. "I told you before the ceremony that I wanted you to have a set of rings this week instead of that borrowed one, so I'd like to take care of it today."

Fay glanced at the antique band on her ring finger as she took the bowl to help herself. "Something like this will do. I don't need anything fancier."

She chose the fruit she wanted and passed the bowl back to him, hoping that put an end to talk of going to Coulter City.

"So you're hot to get back to work," he concluded mildly and she gave a silent nod. "Won't folks over at your place think it's strange for you to show up this quick? To work like today's no different than any other day?"

Fay paused, a fork of melon partway to her mouth. She hadn't thought of that. And of course, Chase pressed on.

"Last night you were worried that the only things folks would see between us are lease agreements and dollar signs. Either last night put a stop to worries like that or—and this'd be my pick—last night's got you running scared."

Fay started to take the bite of melon anyway, but stopped, too irritated to stay silent. "What makes you think you're such a know-it-all?"

"I've got more life experience than you, plus I've been around long enough to get a hint or two about what makes you tick."

Fay took the bite of melon and chewed it as she slid her chair back and stood, dropping her napkin beside her full plate. She reached for her coffee cup and had a last sip before she put it down and looked across the table at him, lifting her brows in challenge.

"Are you getting any hints now?"

Chase leaned back in his chair, the glittering look in his eyes telling her he was both amused and attracted. "I guess I need to say 'Adios, see you at supper.'" He paused. "The keys are still in the car out front if you'd like to use it."

Incensed by his unruffled amusement, Fay swung away and stalked from the dining room through the house to the front door where she let herself out.

She told herself it felt good to walk away from Chase and his know-it-all smugness. She told herself it felt even better to take his car to go home, though in truth the fact that he'd offered it to her without reservation dimmed the satisfaction she might have felt if he'd been in a less accommodating mood.

By the time she pulled up at the main house on Sheridan, she had to work especially hard to feel good about coming here. Thank heavens, Margie's car wasn't in the driveway, so she'd have time to herself to calm down and focus on catching up bookwork until she was ready to think about the hash she'd made of her life.

Why she had to chose bookwork was an irritating reminder that she wasn't quite able to face Riley and the men this early, not after Chase had brought the significance of doing such a thing to her attention. Better to show herself in the afternoon at a time they might find more acceptable for a newlywed.

Aggravated her plan for a head-clearing day of hard work had been spoiled, she slammed the car door and went directly into the house to the den to switch on the computer.

By midmorning, Fay found the note Margie had left in the kitchen: *If you're here to read this, I've taken the day off.* Half starved from missing breakfast, Fay made a pot of coffee and fixed a sandwich from the collection of cold cuts Margie kept in the refrigerator before she raided the cookie jar and added a handful of cookies to her plate.

By two o'clock, she was sick of bookwork and leaned back in the desk chair to calculate how soon she could leave the house and get on a horse. By two-fifteen, she was too restless to care what Riley or any of the men thought and grabbed one of her old Stetsons from the mudroom to walk to the stable to saddle Billy.

Fortunately no one was around when

she rode out. The afternoon heat beat down, so there was no chance of a hard ride. Instead she rode parallel to one of the creeks, going in and out of the sparse shade provided by the irregular stands of trees along the bank. Soon enough she reached the spot where the streambed dipped to form a small waterfall made rocky by the river stones Ty and Troy had lugged home and scattered to make the waterfall a little more noisy and dramatic.

The boys had spent hours along this creek when it had been too hot to do much else, wading and sailing boats they'd made on the back patio. They'd had a penchant for standing in the slow stream for long periods of time, leaning down just over the water to catch fish bare-handed. They'd all three spent time here, enjoying the shade and the water and the outdoors.

Fay dismounted and dropped the reins to let Billy nibble at the tender blades of grass on the shallow bank. The heavy rains they'd received a week ago had swollen the creek for a couple days, but the water had settled to its usual level and whatever muddy silt had been left behind had dried to dust.

She took in a deep breath of fresh air, hoping to somehow draw in the essence of the place and find enough peace to sort things out. While she waited to be soothed, birds chirped here and there, and the water trickled pleasantly over the rocks. The breeze rose and fell lightly, stirring the lazy clap of cottonwood leaves that hung overhead, but all the sounds and scenery seemed to do was highlight the turmoil she felt.

She was in over her head with Chase, and the only thing she'd been able to do about it was run home like the cranky, self-involved female she'd become. The bouts of angry depression she'd lapsed into the past year had suddenly and unexpectedly evolved into a foolish series of bad decisions.

Now she was stuck with a business marriage, *a marriage of convenience,* that was already proving to be upsettingly inconvenient. She'd been an idiot to think she could marry Chase and still have everything her way. She'd meant for him to shake up her life, but only in small doses just challenging enough to distract her from the pain of life without her brothers, but not challenging enough to rock the world.

Memories of the night before threatened, and the will it took to keep them at bay was another sign that she was in over her head. If only she'd insisted on separate rooms, if only she'd vetoed that late supper with the little plastic bride and groom…if only she'd had sense enough to laugh at Chase's first suggestion of marriage and banish it from her mind. If only she'd had the foresight to amend those traditional vows to something she could handle.

Memories of last night finally pierced through her list of regrets, sending a cascade of warmth through her insides that pooled low and took the edge off her raw feelings. It was still hard to believe that a man as big and powerful as Chase could be that tender. He'd taken her to realms of physical pleasure she hadn't dreamed existed, mind shattering places that had brought her to tears, showered her with sweetness, and made her feel whole.

She'd felt something inside her bond to something inside him then, and she suddenly realized she'd been struggling against that particular memory from the moment she'd awakened that morning.

Fay gave an unladylike snort as she finally acknowledged the bitter truth and remembered Chase's guess that morning: *Last night's got you running scared...*

Hell, yes, she was scared. She'd lost her family. She'd loved them all deeply, but instead of having a lifetime with them, she'd lost them all, every one of them. It didn't take a genius to figure she had some kind of dark cloud over her, some deadly jinx. What person in their right mind would want to chance having another family that could be wiped out in a handful of years?

And yet as stupid as it was, she'd put herself smack in the running to allow history another chance at her. She should have known better; there was no excuse for what she'd done. Not hurt, not loneliness, not the craving to be part of a family…

Fay swung from the riverbank to rush toward Billy and grab up his reins in an instinct to outrun the turmoil that churned so wildly inside her.

Whether it was the suddenness of her move alone, or the angry tension she radiated that did it, but Billy threw up his head and shied away. Frustrated, and too riled at herself and the mess she'd made to contain herself, Fay again grabbed for Billy's trailing reins, her quick move uncharacteristically threatening to the big horse who shied again then bolted out of the trees away from her.

Fay's sharp, "Hey!" sealed the sorrel's decision and he burst into a ground-eating gallop across the pasture in the direction of the headquarters.

Stunned, frustrated and suddenly stuck with a two-mile walk home, Fay felt her anger go white-hot, and she stomped her way up the bank.

Cowboy boots weren't good for long walks in the heat, and Fay's feet had broken blisters by the time she got back to the stable and had a good long drink from the outdoor spigot. She found Billy standing outside his stall, still saddled. At least no one had seen him come in riderless and sent out a search party for her. The last thing she was in the mood for was to have everyone find out she'd lost her horse—*again!*—and this time had to walk home.

As worn-out as she was from the heat, she unsaddled Billy and gave him a quick grooming before she put him back in his stall with a bucket of fresh water. Her wrangler would make sure the horse got his measure of grain when he fed the other working horses, and Fay made it to the house before any of the men got back.

She ended up drinking most of a quart of cold water when she reached the house. She'd pried her boots off on the bootjack in the mudroom, so she stopped in the den on her way upstairs for her shower.

There were no messages on her answering machine and no calls from R/K Ranch listed on her caller ID, and Fay felt glum about that, too. Chase had evidently decided to let her pout without interruption and she hated that she felt let down. She walked through the silent house to the stairs, and now that she was calm and tired enough, sadness seemed to waft out from every corner of the house and drag her down.

On the way upstairs, she couldn't help but again compare her home unfavorably to the life and energy of the Rafferty ranch house, and had a fresh struggle with the disloyalty she felt.

She finally walked the length of the upstairs hall and stopped in the open doorway of the boys' room. The large double room had only been dusted and vacuumed in the past year. Not a thing had been moved or boxed away someplace. Everything remained just as Ty and Troy had left it, right down to a partly open closet door, the dresser drawer not quite shut and the comforter that laid a little crookedly on Troy's bed.

Fay leaned against the door frame, sick about marrying Chase so rashly. She hadn't given much thought to her home besides ensuring it would eventually go to someone who would preserve it, whether that someone was Chase or some child they might eventually have.

She'd assumed that since this marriage was business she might be able to go on living here by herself part of the time, but it hadn't taken twenty-four hours to derail that assumption. Chase really wasn't the kind of man who would have agreed to separate dwellings, she should have known that. His "start as you mean to go" declaration didn't allow for much besides the usual marital expectations.

But whether she'd lived with him on the R/K, or they both lived here, Fay realized now that neither arrangement would preserve this last tangible reminder of how and where the boys had lived. At some point, the contents of this room would need to be boxed and put away to make room for the living. Her heart shrank at the thought, but eventually her low feelings lifted enough to remind her it was getting late.

CHAPTER SEVEN

BY 8:00 p.m. she was on her way back to the R/K. Chase still hadn't called or come after her, and it was late enough now that he likely wouldn't. He might be angry, though. From what he'd pointed out to her that morning about how things would look if she showed up for work as usual, he'd probably taken a dim view of his new bride's long absence on their first full day of marriage.

The long walk in the afternoon heat had dried up a significant amount of excess pride and leached away most of her anger, and she'd finally decided she had to stop torturing herself with regret about marrying Chase. It might take a long time to make peace with what she'd done, but she was already sick of the turmoil it caused.

For better or worse. In spite of the foolish decision she'd made to marry Chase, she'd spoken the time-honored vows. The deed was done and now honor required her to live up to what marital expectations she could. Except for the love part. She was willing to care about Chase and make an effort to be a good wife, but love wasn't something she was ready to face, not for a long time to come, if ever.

After visiting the boys' room, she'd decided she'd try to get used to the idea of having children. Once upon a time, she'd looked forward to being married and having children of her own. The difference now was that if she could get past her fear, she'd want at least two children. More than two if she could, because there had to be some safety in numbers. Though she was trying to make new decisions that were more sensible than the ones she'd been making, she didn't entirely escape her low feelings over the rash decisions she'd made until she'd turned off the highway and started down the long driveway on the R/K. Her spirits began to rise the tiniest bit and the heaviness she'd felt began to ease. By the time she pulled Chase's car into the circular front driveway, she felt closer to normal than she'd felt for a long, long time.

Did this mean that the year of heavy grief was beginning to lift? Something warm began to flicker in her chest, and she realized she wanted to see Chase again, though she felt a companion ripple of caution. She didn't want a repeat of last night, not yet. It wouldn't be wise to take too many more risks of pregnancy between now and her doctor's appointment next week. Her life was in enough uproar that she couldn't face pregnancy this soon.

Determined to find some way to keep Chase at arm's length without making the issue a challenge he'd want to take on, Fay got out of the car walked to the house to let herself in. Since she'd already showered at home and changed her clothes, she went in search of Chase. When she realized he was in the den, she took a fortifying breath and walked in as casually as she could.

Chase looked up from the notation he'd made on a pad of paper next to his keyboard. "Welcome home, Mrs. Rafferty," he said mildly. "Ilsa left some supper in the warming oven, unless Margie already fed you."

"Margie took the day off."

Chase tossed down his pen and leaned back in his desk chair, his gaze going over her as if seeking some sign of how she'd spent her day. Other than the change of clothes and the sandals she'd worn home to accommodate a few blisters, which he wouldn't be looking for, she doubted he could tell much about how her day had gone. His question confirmed that.

"Was your day a good one?"

"I'm not sure I'd call it good, but I had time to think."

Chase gave a slow nod. "You look tired."

Rather than acknowledge his remark, she went directly to the apology she owed him. If he'd been the one to go off in a snit and stay away over twelve hours without a word, she'd be livid.

"I'm sorry about today. I should have explained that I needed time to myself."

Now a faint smile eased onto his lips. "And you hate it when I'm right."

She deserved to hear that, but it stirred a bit of spirit. "That, too, but if I were you

I wouldn't get too full of myself." She made a small gesture toward the open door to the family room and the kitchen beyond. "Mind if I bring a plate in?"

"Go on ahead. I'll join you as soon as I finish here."

Fay gave a stiff nod, not certain things were completely smoothed out between them. To tell the truth, she'd expected something a little more difficult, but as she walked out on her way to the kitchen, she realized she should be grateful it had been easy. Her feet hurt, and she was so tired that if she'd been at home, she might have eaten a quick supper and gone straight to bed.

She was too tired to eat quickly, but by the time she'd finished and put her tableware in the dishwasher, Chase still hadn't joined her. Figuring he'd gotten busy again and forgot the time, she turned off the kitchen lights and went to the master suite.

The bed was doubly inviting to a weary mind and body, so Fay went to get a nightgown from one of her suitcases. She hadn't unpacked yet so she took a couple of moments to do it now, stowing her underthings in one of the empty drawers built in on the side of the closet opposite Chase's clothes. She hung up the rest, but tossed her work jeans onto a low shelf. Her toiletries were already in the bathroom cabinet so she closed the suitcases and set them out of the way in a corner of the big closet.

Her nightgown was a soft cotton print with wide shoulder straps, something to wear to bed that was substantial enough to wear around the house without a robe, but hardly sexy or alluring. Once she changed into it, she went in to brush her teeth.

When she came out of the bathroom, there was still no sign of Chase so she went to the patio doors to look out. The square of light that showed on the patio stones just past the center of the house indicated Chase was still in the den. Too tired to be anything but relieved, she drew the drapes and crossed the room to switch on one of the bedside lamps before she climbed into bed.

She tried to stay awake at first, but the emotional turmoil of the day had exhausted her and she felt herself sink into deep sleep.

Chase had meant to join Fay an hour ago, but the program error he'd found demanded clearing up. By the time he was satisfied no information had been lost and he'd backed up everything, he realized it was late.

Now he walked through the big house, turning off the few lights left on. The low light from the end of the hall in the family wing drew him like a moth, and anticipation hit his bloodstream like a drug.

But the moment he saw that his bride

was deeply asleep, he felt a sharp nick of disappointment. It was probably for the best since she'd obviously worn herself out, but his body rebelled at the idea. By the time he slid into bed beside her he'd managed to rein in the natural urge to repeat their wedding night.

He'd just dragged the covers up when she stirred and turned toward him. Whether that was because of a subconscious need to ward him off or the instinct of a woman to gravitate toward her man, he couldn't guess. It was nice, though, to look at her sleep-flushed face, to marvel at how vulnerable she looked without her defenses up, to see her in a peaceful state.

His breath caught when she stirred again and pushed her hand across the sheet toward him. When her fingers encountered his chest, her hand stopped and she mumbled something he couldn't catch. The feel of those slim fingers against his skin set off a slow rising heat that made him pull her against him in a misguided effort to appease it with at least that much. When she sighed and slipped her arm around his waist, he realized his mistake.

It took real effort to slow the beat of his blood and calm his body. The possessiveness he felt toward Fay was strong and heady. The urge to make her his again, to reassure himself that he still had some power over this very independent, strong-willed lady, was intense. It was also a reminder that he'd never needed to win a woman once he'd made love to her. Having sex had been both the proof that the lady had been won and the surprising beginning of the end of the relationship.

It was the opposite with Fay. He reached up and pulled a lock of dark hair off her forehead to smooth it back. The tender feelings she stirred in him came from someplace deep. Of all the women he'd known, she was by far one of the strongest. The idea that one of the strongest was also the one most in need of tenderness got to him and stirred every protective instinct he had.

He pulled her a little more snugly against himself and gave a long sigh of his own before he realized the lamp was still on and it needed to go off.

Fay awoke just after 4:00 a.m., relieved to see that Chase was too deeply asleep to realize she had an arm draped around his middle and a leg wrapped around his hip. Leery of waking him, she carefully eased her arm and leg away and slowly rolled over to scoot to the edge of the mattress.

Thanking heaven for the plain little nightgown that spared her from a repeat of the embarrassing show she'd put on yesterday morning, she walked silently to the bathroom and quietly closed the door. By the time she'd finished in there and slipped into the closet to dress for the day she still hadn't heard any sounds from the bedroom.

She tiptoed out, ruing the prickly pain of broken blisters inside the socks she wore. She'd have to get her boots out of the car later, but she was happy to go without them and spare her feet a little longer.

Figuring the alarm clock on Chase's side of the bed was set to go off, she let herself out of the bedroom and walked more normally to the kitchen. Ilsa hadn't arrived yet, but the coffeemaker was already set up, so Fay switched it on.

The moment it brewed enough coffee to fill a cup, Fay poured it into a heavy mug from the cupboard then walked over to look out the sliding glass doors to the patio. The early light was already growing stronger and the need to be out in the fresh air drew her outdoors. One of the porch swings looked inviting, and she sat down there, leaning back to savor a second sip of coffee.

It had been ages since she'd been content to just sit and enjoy the early morning but it was remarkably easy here. The well-watered flowers and vines were colorful and lush even in the early dawn. The sight of them was soothing and they seemed to radiate a vigor that connected to something in her that she hadn't felt for a long time.

Almost immediately she thought of Ty and Troy, but as she braced her heart for a fresh spasm of hard grief, she felt instead a bittersweet ache. The thought that they'd be too eager for a fast start on the day to be able to sit around in the relative cool of dawn caused the ache to deepen only a little.

She still missed them, but somehow the peace and beauty of the early morning made it easier to remember them without being stricken down. For the first time since the accident, she had the distinct sense that they truly were safe with God in his heaven. Though she'd tried to console herself with that knowledge early on, her heart had rebelled so violently against their loss that she'd been unable to grasp it however hard she'd tried. The sense of death had been oppressively heavy back then and had permeated every thought, stifling everything good or hopeful.

But suddenly in the peace and sweetness of that moment her heart was certain, and with that knowledge something deep and painful in her heart began to lose some of its power and sting. The boys lives hadn't come to nothing. They still lived somewhere beyond the sunrise, and for the first time in a very long time she realized the bitterness she'd held was beginning to ease.

She'd never know why she'd lost them so soon, and acknowledged to herself that even if she'd been given an explanation she might not have been able to accept it.

How long she sat there lost in memory, pondering a lifetime of the teachings of her parents and their country church, she didn't know. When she finally realized the sun hovered level with the horizon and that its light was beginning to pierce the shadows and unlock more colorful flower blossoms, she had a last look around and remembered why she was here at this early hour.

She'd married Chase Rafferty. The reminder was a lot less shocking than it had been yesterday and the day before. Maybe she hadn't made too big a mess of her life, but only time would settle that. Feeling calm inside and more optimistic about life than she'd felt for a long time, she got up out of the swing determined to cling to those feelings as she carried her lukewarm coffee into the kitchen.

Ilsa's immediate, "G'morning, I see you

like that swing as much as I do," was warm and pleasant and Fay smiled.

"Good morning. It's nice out there."

"It's still early yet, but once the sun's fully up it'll be time for the hummingbirds to start their rounds. We've got two females nesting near the top of the vines, but I don't know where the others keep themselves."

They chatted a few minutes before Fay emptied her coffee cup and set it in the sink. She carried the tray of tableware and the coffee carafe to the dining room where Chase was sitting with the newspaper spread out on the glossy table before him.

When she came in, he moved the paper out of the way, turning to the side a little as he kept reading. She was still in her sock feet and without the sound of her boots he probably thought she was Ilsa. Fay set the tray down and poured a cup of steaming coffee that she sat in his side vision, then watched him reach for the cup and do a double-take as she set his plate and silverware next to it.

He immediately closed the paper but stayed silent as he watched her set the table. When she finished and picked up the tray, he spoke.

"Aren't you forgetting something, Mrs. Rafferty?"

The sexy smile that played around his mouth was thoroughly...likable. She knew he was hinting at a morning kiss, but instead she glanced at the place settings before she looked over at him.

"I can't think of a thing, Mr. Rafferty." With that, she carried the tray to the kitchen. The sharp rustle of the newspaper behind her was meant as wordless protest but she pretended to ignore it.

Ilsa let her carry in the tray with their breakfast. When she walked in to the dining room Chase briskly closed and refolded his paper to put it aside as she set out the food. When she passed behind him, she paused only long enough to lean down to kiss his razor smooth cheek before she went on around the table to sit. Chase half rose from his chair in a gesture of politeness until she was seated, but when he caught her gaze the male interest and intensity in his eyes made it hard to break contact.

"Something's new, isn't it?" He said it like a statement rather than a question and his gaze narrowed as he studied her a moment. "You either colored your hair or...you got up on the right side of the bed."

Pleased with himself, he passed her the meat platter and reached for his napkin to unfold it and drop it to his lap. Fay helped herself to a breakfast steak and handed back the platter.

"There's nothing worse than a joker at the breakfast table," she replied as she slipped four over-easy eggs onto her plate and doused them with as many splashes of hot sauce. Chase picked up the egg platter but eyed her plate with mock suspicion as he helped himself to the rest of the eggs.

"I meant to ask again about spending a little time together today," he said as he set the empty platter aside, "but if you're really going to eat those eggs maybe I should just shut up and eat."

Fay lifted a forkful of egg to her mouth before she reached with her free hand to turn the hot sauce bottle so he could read the label. Chase obliged.

"Mild, huh?" He gave her a narrow look.

Fay shrugged. "You're the one who bragged that he's got more life experience than I do and some idea of what makes me tick. So, how'm I ticking now?"

The twinkle in his gaze told her he was pleased with their exchange. "Something tells me I need to watch what I say in the future."

"Very good," she said, feeling a quiver of enjoyment that had the potential to mushroom, and she wasn't sure she was quite ready for that. She tried to put an end to it. "What did you have in mind for today?" Her change of subject was too abrupt and she could tell Chase had noticed. He adopted a less playful air and Fay suddenly regretted her cowardice.

"The same thing I had in mind yesterday," he began, "only I can get the jeweler to come out here if you'd rather. I'd like to give you a paper overview of the R/K so you're at least familiar with a few things, but we don't have to do that today. Before we do an overview, I thought we might take a truck out, let you get your bearings over here."

Fay answered him honestly. "I need to be on a horse, at least until it heats up."

He nodded. "You and I think alike there."

The brief moments of playfulness between them combined with Chase's natural masculine appeal, and the old attraction she'd thought was long gone stirred hard as they finished breakfast in companionable silence. After Chase chivalrously got her boots from the car, they walked down to the stable and Fay began to feel the need to be cautious with him.

She already felt a bond to Chase that went beyond the fact that they'd been intimate. That mysterious bond was almost too much as it was, and she wasn't sure she wanted to even flirt with the idea of more. She could be comfortable with friendship, she could accept intimacy, especially now that she realized one taste of it made her willing for more, but it was falling in love with Chase that she was afraid of.

Her persistent cowardice about that was beginning to need some shoring up as they rode along a long flat ridge that ran above a shallow valley. They were both too competitive to ride side by side for long before they somehow began to race. Fay instantly nudged her horse into the lead, relishing his power beneath her and the wind on her face. The warm morning air pulled at her shirt, riffling the cotton and making her glad she'd tugged her hat down firmly when they'd started to run.

A glance at Chase showed him leaning low over his horse's neck, the iron set of his jaw pure macho determination as he slowly gained on her and they rode neck and neck. When he dropped his hand to the horse's neck to urge the big gray to move into the lead, Fay remembered the feel of that firm hand and felt a harsh stir of desire so far out of context in a horse race that a gurgle of laughter burst up and she was suddenly in danger of falling out of the saddle.

She rapidly realized she couldn't keep up and began to ease back on the reins to slow the relentless stride of her horse. The bay she'd chosen was reluctant to allow the gray to speed on, and the short battle of wills sobered her long enough to slow him down.

Chase rode on, oblivious to the fact that she'd broken off the race. For once in what felt like years, laughter so caught her up that she was in even more danger of falling off her horse, and Fay pulled harder on the reins to slow the bay to a quick trot then a ground-eating walk. The horse snorted his displeasure and Fay leaned forward to pat his neck, giggling out an apology.

It felt so good to laugh again at something, even if it was mostly at herself, and now the fact that Chase was a good half mile ahead of her and still churning ground seemed even more hilarious. A moment more and she saw him glance over his shoulder and pull back on the reins as he straightened in the saddle. The gray slowed enough to run in a long, wide arc to circle back.

By then Fay's laughter had bubbled away and she'd finally pulled her horse to a fidgeting stop. When the big animal reared a little, she got a sure indication of his impatience and urged him into a trot before she turned him toward the east to ride at an easy lope.

Chase's gray caught up and gave a gusty snort before he slowed enough to match the bay's stride. Fay couldn't seem to stop smiling. The morning was the best one she'd had for a long time and she was alive with the simple richness of it.

A quick glance toward Chase showed her he'd caught a sense of the pleasure she felt and he gestured toward another slow rise and angled his horse in that direction. Fay rode after him till they reached the top and rode into a wide, shallow valley marked down the center with a long line of cottonwoods. A thin creek bed ran through the trees.

Chase slowed his horse to a walk and she slowed hers. By the time they reached the creek and turned to ride parallel to it to cool their horses, a deep sense of companionship wove between them and their ongoing silence was as satisfying as it was comfortable. By the time they could stop, they'd reached a thickening in the tree line and Chase led the way down the bank to a wide spot in the creek.

They each dismounted and when Chase stripped the saddle off his horse, Fay did the same. Both animals deserved a cool drink and some rest in the shade. Fay felt invigorated by the ride but the sight and sound of the creek was calming. She wouldn't mind shucking off her boots and cooling her blistered feet in the water, so she sat down on the ground and pulled off her boots and socks, then proceeded to roll up her jeans' legs.

Chase towered nearby holding the horses' reins out of the way as the pair noisily had a drink of creek water. After a minute, he led them away from the water's edge and pulled a pair of rope hobbles off his saddle.

Fay rested her arms on her bent knees and watched as he hunkered down to apply the hobbles. When he straightened, he took off both bridles and laid them on his saddle as the horses lowered their heads and began to nibble at the shaded grass.

Fay lifted her gaze to Chase as he walked over and sat down next to her on the grass. He pulled off his hat and tossed it aside as he leaned on an elbow to stretch out. The silence between them was rich with the sound of the chattering creek and the sound of the horses. Birds twittered here and there and the other sounds that had stopped when they'd arrived began to start again.

"I want to make love to you."

Chase's low words, blunt as they were, fit into the other sounds around them as naturally as if they belonged there. Fay turned her head in surprise and found her gaze captured by his as he reached to pull her down beside him. The moment he touched her she felt herself sway toward him, and any thought she might have had to resist melted away.

CHAPTER EIGHT

IN SPITE of Fay's natural caution about falling in love with Chase, those next days and weeks settled into a pattern of companionship that slowly began to chip away at the grief and secret loneliness of the past year. Chase made a deep impact on her, challenging and cajoling her out of the twilight of a solitary existence and wordlessly daring her more fully into the bright dawn of a new life.

Almost right away Fay discovered that making love to Chase was very nearly that: making love. Pride demanded she not be such a pushover, but by the time she could again convince herself she was immune to him, Chase touched her or gave her that special, lingering glance, and her determination to keep him at a less tempting distance melted away.

It was some comfort that he'd never mentioned the word love in the nearly two months they'd been married. She could easily acknowledge the very natural deep affection she had for him now, but love in any context but the physical one was still safely absent.

It was just a week after the two-month anniversary of their trip to Vegas when they spent a rare day apart. There'd been only a handful of those so far, but this time Fay found it difficult to concentrate. Truth to tell, she'd found it difficult to concentrate for the past week, but today was different.

Chase had flown to Fort Worth with their ranching neighbor, Bob Carson, and Fay thought it was a good opportunity to begin making decisions about which calves she'd offer for sale after the fall gather. Then there was the inevitable bookwork at Sheridan Ranch, and because it was nearing the first of the month, there were bills to pay.

It was after four that afternoon before she finished with everything and drove back to the R/K. When she walked in, she went directly to the master suite to shower and change her clothes. When she finished, she heard Ilsa in the kitchen and went out to see her.

"I thought you'd be gone by now, or I would have said hello when I came in," Fay said. Ilsa waved that away then opened a cabinet door to take out her handbag.

"I had a couple of things I wanted to catch up, and it's just as well. Bob's wife called before you got home. She said he and Chase should be back in the next hour."

Fay nodded. They'd been invited to supper with the Carsons, just a casual meal, but she was looking forward to it. "Thanks. I'll be leaving in a few minutes."

"I'll see you in the morning," Ilsa said then walked to the back door.

"See you in the morning," Fay echoed and went back to the master suite to get the small handbag that held little more than a comb and a wallet. The white jeans and red blouse she'd chosen to wear for supper were simple but eye-catching, and a last glance in the mirror called attention to the fact that she'd forgotten to put on her rings.

She went to the dresser tray and picked up the sturdy gold chain that held the rings Chase had insisted on buying her. She opened the clasp and started to take them off. Rings were a hazard for outdoor work, but she wore them on the chain during the day. She'd taken it off for her shower then almost forgotten to put them on before she drove over to the Carsons. Good thing she'd noticed.

Heaven forbid she'd show up anywhere without the showy set of rings Chase had insisted upon. The memory of the last time they'd gone out and he'd discovered she'd forgotten to wear them played in her mind and she was lost for a moment in the blatantly sensual memory.

A smile eased over her lips as she felt desire shiver through her. Heaven forbid was definitely the wrong way to look back at the delicious consequence Chase had dealt her. If they'd simply been going out, she might have hidden the rings in her pocket to tease him, but since they were having supper with neighbors, she slipped them on.

The deep craving to see Chase again, to be with him, came over her with sobering power. It was becoming harder and harder to dismiss her feelings as natural affection and friendship, but she made herself do it now. She was still afraid to allow Chase access to her whole heart.

Though she realized it was illogical to believe that truly loving Chase put not only her heart at risk, but might also open some mysterious door to tragedy, she couldn't seem to completely overcome the idea. Why couldn't she just take life as it came and not see shadows and pitfalls at each step? Impatient with herself, Fay grabbed up her handbag and left the house.

The drive took a good half hour and by the time Fay drove in at the Carson place, Josie was waiting at the front door and came out to join her. Fay parked her car so they could walk together to the open Jeep parked in the lane near the house. Since Bob and Chase were due any minute, they got in to drive out to the small airfield that was just over a mile from the ranch house.

It didn't take long to get caught up on news since the last time they'd been together just over a week ago, and Fay realized how much she enjoyed Josie's company. It had been a good day, despite Chase's absence, and now that they were nearing the landing strip, Fay realized that the day was about to get even better.

Her heart began to beat with anticipation when the lowering sun shone on a small aircraft that was little more than a metallic twinkle in the distance. The excitement she'd tried to push down began to rise higher as the twinkle grew larger. Josie pulled the Jeep to a stop several feet from the side of the runway and switched off the engine.

When the sound died away they almost immediately heard the faint but odd skip of the aircraft engine, and Fay's breath went shallow as she listened harder. The engine slowly grew louder and seemed steady now. Just when she decided she must have imagined the small skip of sound, it happened again and Josie cocked her head the slightest bit, as if she wasn't sure she was hearing right.

A few moments more and there was no mistaking the rough sound of the engine. Josie sent Fay a worried glance as she reached to start the Jeep and back it a safe distance from the side of the landing strip. Now the plane was near enough to clearly hear the irregular hiccup of a failing engine. Suddenly the sound of the engine stopped and the small craft began to drift heavily downward.

Alarmed, Fay stood up in the open Jeep, her heart crowding painfully into her throat as she gripped the top of the windshield. Josie was standing on her seat, her white-knuckled hold on the windshield matching Fay's, only Josie was yelling advice that Bob couldn't possibly hear.

Terror seized her insides, and Fay bit her lip so hard she tasted blood.

Everything moved in slow-motion as the silent plane appeared to hang on an invisible wire, hovering there for fractions of seconds before it slid lower to wobble and hover again thanks to whatever lift an air current or wing flap provided. Fay couldn't look away from the multiplying horror as the plane's descent grew too steep. *Please, God!*

And then the plane wobbled one last time and simply dropped, its nose coming up just before the left landing wheel collapsed to tip the wing down to slice the ground a quarter mile short of the far end of the runway. An explosion of dust accompanied the wrench and boom of metal as the wing tore partially away and the side of the plane hit the dirt. The awful squeal of metal on the ungiving ground tore at her heart and Fay could only watch as the plane plowed over the weedy dirt to a groaning stop.

Smoke and dust boiled up to obscure the unmoving craft and Fay fell backward onto the seat. Whether that was because her legs gave out or because Josie had dropped down behind the wheel and hit the accelerator to race for the far end of the runway, she didn't know. Her hands had lost their grip on the windshield and Fay awkwardly reached up with an arm that felt like lead to hold on to the safety bar on the side of the dashboard.

Just past the end of the runway, Josie jammed on the brakes to stop the vehicle well away from the danger of the plane, tossing them both forward. Josie was the first one out, though Fay wasn't more than a heartbeat behind. Her legs felt abnormally heavy and so unsteady it was a wonder she could run at all. The quarter mile distance seemed to take a lifetime to cross.

Flames began to flicker from the engine

just as Chase fought his way out the door and then reached back in for Bob. Both men disappeared for a terrifying few seconds, and it seemed to take another lifetime before they appeared again from the other side of the wrecked plane, only this time they were lugging fire extinguishers. In seconds, twin bursts of fire retardant smothered the flames and heavily frosted the crumpled metal.

Bob turned and dropped his fire extinguisher just in time for Josie to launch herself at him, catching him around the neck to kiss him wildly. Bob let out a joyful whoop and lifted Josie off the ground to swing her in a circle.

Fay's legs were almost too heavy and weak to take her the whole distance to Chase, but he moved toward her to catch her up. Fay couldn't hang onto him hard enough as she tightened her arms around his neck, reveling in the solid, strong feel of his big body. He was alive and whole, and though some of the horror of the crash receded a little, terror had already gotten a painful grip.

"I was so a-afraid," she babbled into the cotton cloth that stretched across his shoulder. Chase's arms were all but crushing her.

"Sorry, darlin'."

"Are you really all right?" She leaned away from Chase enough to see his face. She pulled an arm from around his neck to catch his chin and hold his head still for a good long look. A cut oozed near his hairline. Once she saw that, she slid her hands between them and pushed back enough to look over the rest of him. Skinned knuckles and a tear in the arm of his shirt were the only other signs of injury, but the skin underneath the tear was unmarked.

"Just a scratch or two," he said, and Fay

searched his eyes. The steady "all there" look was reassuring, but she was too shaken up to grasp it. *She'd almost lost him.* That he'd survived the plane crash miraculously unharmed didn't seem to gain much headway against the idea that he'd come so close to losing his life. The sick feeling that had gripped her from the moment they'd realized there was trouble with the plane began to thicken.

The hysterical notion of being some sort of jinx made a strong pass through her thoughts as Chase tucked her against his side and the four of them started for the Jeep. Fay walked along with her arm tight around Chase's lean middle, trapped in a dizzy haze of sick anxiety as she listened to Bob and Chase recount the flight and details of the crash.

A couple of pickup trucks and a tractor hauling a water wagon were speeding across the pasture toward the airstrip. Bob issued orders to the first two ranch hands who arrived, then started to get behind the wheel of the Jeep.

"No, you don't, Bobby," Josie declared as she gave him a playful shove toward the back of the Jeep. "Momma's drivin' now," she said and got in. Fay got in on the passenger side and Chase climbed into the back next to Bob.

"I'm in the doghouse now," Bob called out, then broke into a badly sung line from an old Country Western song with the same line. Josie giggled and started the Jeep to pull it forward into a turn that sent them back toward the headquarters.

Fay sat silent, realizing how much comfort she'd taken from Chase's touch only now that they were separated by a couple of feet. The craving to be close to him, to be as close to him as was humanly possible, crashed through her. *She'd almost lost him.* The thought repeated in her brain like a dirge that made the sick feelings grow heavy.

The dread she'd carried around for what seemed like forever had taken a fresh grip, and she simply couldn't make it fade.

Back at the house they all trooped into the kitchen. Chase and Bob washed up in the downstairs bathroom while Fay and Josie washed up in the kitchen. Josie hadn't said much to her, but as she handed Fay a tea towel to dry her hands, she spoke up.

"I'm sorry you saw that, Fay. If I'd even thought—"

"You couldn't have known," she said, then made herself smile. And though she felt dishonest trying to make a joke of it, she did it anyway. "It's a good thing all they did was crash a plane. If a horse had been involved, they could have been hurt."

Josie laughed at that, but there was a watchfulness in her gaze that made Fay glance away and told her Josie could tell she was trying too hard. Josie hung her tea towel and looped a friendly arm around her shoulder. “None of us know how long we’ve got, Fay. The best we can do is make the most of every day we get.”

Though the bit of wisdom was true, Fay shook her head. “I know. It’s just that…I must be greedy.”

Josie gave her a hard hug. “I know. Me, too.” She drew back. “Bob’s not going out of this house without me for at least a month,” she declared with a smile.

Determined to buck up and not be such a baby, Fay gave an answering smile she hoped didn’t look too fake.

The informal supper turned into more a party for dozens than it did supper for four. First it was a neighbor who’d heard Bob’s plane go over, then it was the sheriff, and then other flying buddies of Bob’s came by. A TV news crew arrived to take some film of the crashed plane and do a short interview with Bob just before dark, and sometime after nine that evening a flying friend from Coulter City, who was also a doctor, stopped by.

Josie had called him, just to be sure the bump on the head Bob had taken was okay and that Chase's cut didn't need stitches. Fay was relieved Josie had done that, despite their minor injuries. She suspected then that Josie had been putting on a brave front all evening.

At long last they were on their way home. Chase was driving, and Fay was glad. Her body was still reacting to the brutal surprise of the crash, and in spite of eating a good meal, the nausea that had struck her earlier had returned with a vengeance to make her weak and more than a little miserable.

Finally they were back at the R/K and

Fay went to the master suite to get ready for bed. Chase had gone to the den to check for messages, so she changed into her nightgown. That's when the nausea that had plagued her grew acute and she rushed into the bathroom.

Thank heaven Chase was in the den and wouldn't find out she was still this worked up. He'd already apologized, more than once, for putting her through the crash.

Remembering that now made her want to cry. The idea that he'd apologized for something he couldn't help made her heart ache. *She loved him so much.*

The thought exploded into her mind. *She loved Chase so much.* Surprise sent a fresh quake of shock through her heart and Fay made herself walk to the sink. She leaned down and dashed her face with cold water, as if she could dash away the thought as easily.

She loved him so much.

A wave of unhappiness went through her and Fay sagged wearily against the sink. After a few moments, she pushed herself upright and reached for a towel to blot her face. She couldn't be in love with Chase, not really. She only thought she was now because the crash had upset her so much.

It was just too soon after Ty and Troy had been killed. Surely the reason she thought she was in love with Chase was because the crash had stirred up memories of the very worst time in her life. Her emotions had been traumatized afresh, and the idea that she'd fallen in love with Chase had to be part of the maelstrom of a second trauma coming so close to the first.

Fay's stomach finally calmed enough to brush her teeth. She went straight to bed then laid there, her brain too busy to let her sleep. And then Chase walked in and the craving to touch him again, to somehow reassure herself that he was truly all right made her impatient for him to take a quick shower. When he slid into bed next to her and switched off the lamp, she couldn't keep from pressing into his arms.

CHAPTER NINE

FAY spent that next week in private misery. Words she hadn't wanted to think, much less say, had slipped out the night of the crash.

I love you. She'd only said them once—she was *fairly* certain it had only been once—but Chase hadn't seemed to notice. Their lovemaking that night had carried an edge of desperation, a compulsion to drive away the remnants of terror and reaffirm life. They hadn't made love quite like that before, and somewhere in the middle of it all, the words had slipped out.

Had Chase even heard them? Until he'd gotten into bed, he hadn't given a hint that the crash had shaken him up. She should have known his lack of seriousness about it had been part of the macho pride of males who suffered their close calls with good humor, hard drinking, or bar brawls, but the night of the crash she'd learned macho males also channeled their reactions into mind-blowing sex. Mind-blowing enough to drive their women to admit things better left unsaid.

Now she was torn between wishing the words hadn't come out and worrying because Chase hadn't said them to her. She'd begun to make peace with the idea that she was in love with him, but there was no peace at all in the idea that he might not love her.

Her bullheaded determination never to fall in love had been given a comeuppance she hadn't anticipated, and the scope of her self-centered perspective shamed her. It had never crossed her conceited mind that Chase might never love her, and now the joke was on her.

Their lovemaking since that night became even more frequent than it had been before. They also worked longer hours than normal, leaving little time for talk. Even mealtimes were more silent than usual until their days seemed to amount to little more than work and sex.

And yet Fay's time away from Chase wasn't quite as full of hard work as she let on. Her reaction to the shock of the crash had lingered, and she felt sick off and on during the day. She'd rarely been oversensitive to the heat, and she'd hardly ever had days when hard work wore her out to the point of needing an afternoon nap, but now the heat sapped her well before noon, and she fell asleep in the den after lunch.

At least she felt better by midafternoon, and each time she'd decide her reaction to the crash was finally over until the next day in late morning when she'd feel sick and dizzy and weak enough to drag herself to the house again.

By the second week after the crash, she made up her mind to fight this bout of nerves. She would put up with the heat, she'd keep working through the nausea and the weakness, and force herself to keep going until the bad nerves finally wore themselves out. It seemed like a good plan in the cool of early morning, but by the time the sun was high, only sheer force of will kept her in the saddle as she hazed the last of the cattle through a pasture gate to fresh grass.

Thank God she was almost done, and it was close enough to the noon meal that she could go to the house. It was a good thing she was riding Blackie, a steady older horse who didn't have an excitable bone in his body. He was such an old hand at moving cattle that he did all the work while she kept a bloodless grip on the saddle horn and toughed it out.

The last cow was through the gate by the time the heat and the nausea combined with the dizziness she felt and made her lean to the side to be deeply and profoundly sick. As if he'd been expecting it, Blackie came to a slow halt and stood patiently. Once the sickness passed, Fay straightened and nudged him forward so she could catch the corner of the gate.

A veteran at closing gates, Blackie turned and walked calmly in a half circle until Fay could push the gate closed and lean down to shove the latch into place. The dizziness all but pulled her from the saddle when she did that, but Fay managed to hang on and right herself.

She felt so, so sick, and closed her eyes for long moments as she waited for the world to stop spinning. As soon as she could, she turned Blackie toward home and he moved into a sedate walk that she deeply appreciated.

Fay stopped him partway to rinse her mouth and have a few sips of water from her canteen. Thankfully the water settled her stomach, but she was careful to limit the amount. When the buildings of the headquarters came into sight she began to feel only a little better, and decided then that she'd drive to Coulter City after her nap to see the doctor. She'd had enough of this nonsense. Either she was truly sick and needed some kind of medicine or treatment, or she needed something for her nerves. Whatever the reason, she was done feeling so bad.

Fay dismounted inside the stable, clinging to the saddle while she waited for her knees to stop shaking. By the time she was certain she could walk, her wrangler came in and she handed Blackie off to be unsaddled and groomed. Though she rarely did that, she couldn't have managed the task, and it was all she could do to walk from there to the house.

When she got inside to the air-conditioning, she pried her boots off on the bootjack, then walked into the kitchen, reviving a little in the cool air as she stopped at the sink and soaped her hands and face to wash up. Margie came in as she dried her hands.

"Land sakes, you're lookin' white as a sheet!" Margie rushed over to take Fay's arm and gently lead her to the kitchen table. Fay was too wrung-out to protest and was grateful to sit down.

"What's the matter, honey, are you sick?" Margie's face was the picture of concern and Fay gave her a faint smile.

"I guess so. I'm hungry, though."

Margie put out a hand and pressed her palm to her forehead. "Well, you're hot, but you just came in from the heat. We ought to make sure you're not dehydrated." With that, Margie went to the refrigerator for the pitcher of ice water and got a glass out of the cupboard to bring back.

Fay had a few sips then set the glass aside. "Is lunch ready?" She glanced hopefully toward the stove, but nothing was cooking.

"You look like you oughta settle for chicken broth and crackers," Margie declared and marched to the pantry. She brought back a box of saltines that she set on the table in front of Fay before she stepped to the refrigerator again and opened the freezer compartment to rummage around.

"Good thing I froze some chicken stock."

Fay opened a package of saltines and pulled out a half dozen squares, suddenly ravenous. She'd worked her way through half the paper sleeve before Margie set a deep bowl of broth in front of her along with a napkin and spoon.

"Go slow on that till you see how it sets. It might be a little too rich."

Fay picked up the spoon and dug in, her taste buds perking up at the taste. She tossed in a few saltines and made a meal of the simple combination. Margie left the kitchen to finish what she'd been doing before she came back and sat down across from Fay in time to see her take the last spoonful of broth. A moment later, Fay realized Margie was staring thoughtfully at her.

The cool air and the broth had revived her and she smiled. "Am I still pale?"

Margie shook her head. "Nope." She kept studying Fay's face, hinting she wanted to say more.

"What is it?"

"Nothing. You still oughta see that doctor."

Fay's smile slipped. "I think I agree, though I don't feel bad now. Just tired." Margie nodded.

"Then why don't you go lie down a while? I'll give the doc a call, see if he can work you in before he closes. That'll give you time to rest and clean up."

Fay stood, feeling better but so tired she really did need that nap. "Thanks, Margie."

"Sure thing," the woman said, and got up to go to the phone.

Fay walked out of the doctor's office late that afternoon in a daze, and though she hadn't been sick again, she was in far worse shape than she'd been in the past week or so. The prescription in her handbag made a stop at the pharmacy a must, and she welcomed the added time in Coulter City before she had to get back to the R/K.

She drove to the pharmacy, but once she handed over the prescription slip to the pharmacist, she wandered the store aisles trying to interest herself in the merchandize and distract herself from the doctor's diagnosis. Eventually her eye caught on a revolving rack of medical pamphlets with a stand of health-related books next to it.

She glanced over the titles, eventually daring to pick up a specific one. The thick hardcover was heavy and she noticed her hands were shaking. Curiosity was just about the only thing that persuaded her to keep holding the book.

Everything You Want To Know About Pregnancy And Childbirth, Plus A Few Things You Might Not.

The word "pregnancy" assaulted her eyeballs with a little of the force that the doctor's words had struck her heart.

"You're not sick, Fay, you're pregnant."

She'd been too horrified to object or to demand another test. But then she'd felt an inkling of excitement as the doctor congratulated her and listed a few things that answered questions she'd been too stunned to think of.

Fay carried the book with her to sit near the pharmacist's window to wait while she scanned the table of contents and flipped through the pages.

As the title indicated, the book seemed to cover everything most women would want to know about pregnancy and childbirth. In those few minutes while her emotions rose and whirled, and shifted between excitement and deep, dark dread, she previewed enough of the book—complete with charts, diagrams and vivid photos—to know that even the humorous part, *Plus A Few Things You Might Not,* had no section advising what to do if you were scared to be pregnant and doubly scared that the baby's father wasn't in love with you.

And of course there would be nothing in any of those many pages that could advise her on how to tell Chase about this without triggering an automatic pledge of love from a man who'd mean well, but whose heart wasn't genuinely in love.

By the time her prescription for vitamins was filled and she paid for it and the thick book at the register, she realized she wasn't ready to go back to the R/K, not until she'd calmed down enough to decide how to tell Chase.

Fay drove directly to Sheridan Ranch, glad Margie would be gone for the day so she could have the house to herself. When she got there, she left her purse in the kitchen and walked up the back stairs. The late afternoon sun was streaming in the west windows as she walked down the hall to the boys' room and went in to sit on Troy's bed.

She hadn't sat on his bed in the past year, or on Ty's, but it felt okay to do it now. She looked slowly around the big room, pausing here and there on the mementos and artifacts from two lives lived with the energy and happy excitement of children who had been dearly loved. For the first time she realized that the family that had dwindled to one was now two, and she put a hand to her flat middle in an instinctive need to somehow touch that new life.

She must have gotten pregnant on their wedding night after all. The doctor had laughed at her brief bout of consternation over that. She remembered giggling once over a friend who'd had the same thing happen and remembered now that instead of being upset, her friend had been delirious with joy.

Fay felt the glittering rise of something that felt a whole lot like joy, and her fear about having a child began to ease. In spite of trying to avoid it, a baby had been conceived. The sense that this new life was meant to come now, whether she was ready for it or not, began to settle in.

The peace of the quiet room wrapped around her and she sat there for a long time. It was a while before she realized she'd lapsed into a daydream, wondering what the baby would look like and whether it was a boy or a girl. That she could sit in this room, in this house, and not only feel joy again but to also look toward the future with excitement, was a surprise that released the last of the heavy grief of the past year.

The bittersweet knowledge that her brothers would want her to be happy and live a full life with every bit of the gusto and wonder they'd had, helped her let go of the last of her fears and whatever remained of her secret guilt about outliving them.

By the time she walked back downstairs, Fay was eager to get home. Home. It was literally the first time she'd thought of the R/K as home, and she hurried all the more. She didn't know exactly when she'd tell

Chase about the baby or how, but she suddenly realized she'd know it when the right time came. She walked out to her car and got in, tossing her handbag on the seat next to the bag that held the vitamins and the book before she put on her seat belt and started the engine to drive away from Sheridan Ranch.

It'd been a hell of a day. Chase returned to the house and got cleaned up in a temper born of frustration and the kind of cowardice he would have laughed at two months ago. The source of the very special and only truly tortuous frustration he'd felt in his entire life, suddenly walked into the house a half hour after he did and he could tell she'd been to town.

Fay was dressed in a shiny pink sundress that highlighted her dark hair and made you notice that her eyes were exactly as blue as her dress was pink. The gold sandals she had on showed how small and pretty her feet were, and the short length of her sundress showed off her long, shapely legs. Added to her bare arms, almost bare shoulders, and the way that pink dress cinched in at the waist and called extra attention to that eye-catching little V in front, Fay looked exactly like dessert.

The temper that had been riding him all afternoon cooled a little and he reined in the rest, giving his wife a quick almost chaste kiss before she briefly escaped him to rush her handbag and drugstore sack to their bedroom. When she joined him in the dining room, the smile she gave him was that same slight, flirtatious and yet secretive smile he'd seen more and more these past weeks, a smile that promised to satisfy his every craving if he dared to grab her up and carry her off.

As he seated Fay at her place and went

around the table to sit down, his body started ticking off the moments until he could do just that as Miss Ilsa brought in their supper.

By the time they'd finished eating, his internal timer went off and he tossed his napkin to the table and went around to collect Fay. He picked her up off the chair and ignored her surprise as he called out, "We'll have the rest later, Ilsa," and walked out of the room.

Fay wasn't too surprised by Chase's caveman abduction from the table. He'd done it before and, truth to tell, she loved it. What was different this time was the grim set of his face and the no-nonsense gleam in his eyes that told her he was angry. She couldn't imagine what had set him off, but he'd weathered her tempers often enough that she had no worries about putting up with his.

Besides, she was the last female who

could be cowed or browbeaten by a show of masculine ire, so the only real reaction she felt was curiosity. She held onto his neck as he stalked into their room, paused to kick the door shut, then walked to the bed. He started to lean down to sit her in the middle of the mattress when he stopped.

As if he'd reconsidered, he carried her around the bed to the overstuffed chairs in front of the glass doors to the patio and set her in one of those before he stepped back, his eyes a stormy blue as he glared down at her.

He seemed to notice something about her and narrowed his gaze. Fay wasn't shy about speaking up.

"What? Have I done something?"

He came right back with, "You have."

"And you're angry about it," she guessed, unable to think of a thing she'd done that was worth him being this stirred up. He shook his head and corrected her.

"I'm frustrated. With you, with me. Makes me touchy."

Fay gave a slow nod, trying not to giggle because he'd admitted to being "touchy" instead of angry, when he was almost as angry as she'd ever seen him. She didn't dare laugh because he was so serious. Though she wasn't afraid of his temper, she didn't see a need to provoke him, at least not that way.

"You might as well tell me why, straight out," she said. "When I get 'touchy,' I never make you guess why." She couldn't resist trying to tease him out of his bad mood. "Of course I hardly ever get a chance to make you guess, you being older and more experienced, not to mention how all-knowing you are about what makes me tick."

A smile tugged at the stern line of his mouth. "You're never going to let me off the hook for that remark, are you?" Fay shrugged, delighted that he'd responded just like she'd hoped.

"You've been pretty good about that lately, so I might."

Chase dragged the other overstuffed chair over so it faced hers before he sat down. His mysterious anger seemed to have passed, but she wasn't sure she could identify what she sensed in him now until he went on. "How 'bout I admit that other than a thing or two now and then, that I'm more often…not sure of you?"

His low voice and the way he said that touched her and the playfulness she'd felt leaked away. "Why don't you just ask?" The question seemed to rile him.

"Because I'd sooner face a wild bull in a box than…" The frustration he'd mentioned was evident then and he was on his feet to stalk to the glass doors and glare out. After a few seconds he reached for the drapery cord and gave it an irritable yank that whipped the drapes together and left them swinging. Another moment more and he turned toward her, his blue gaze fiery again as he finished what he'd been about to say.

"Because I'd sooner face a wild bull in a box than lay my heart at the feet of Fay Sheridan Rafferty. To put it in plain English: Did you mean what you said the other night?"

The admission and demand made her straighten in her chair as what he was trying to say began to dawn on her, but she was wary. Now that she'd realized the shameful depth of her self-centeredness and conceit, she was cautious about assuming much of anything, especially something this important.

She hesitated to answer his question right away, in case she was wrong. "The other night? The night of the plane crash?"

"Yes, *that* night, but never mind." He released a harsh breath and seemed to let go of some of his tension. When he spoke again, his voice was low and even, and his words were the kind of blunt in-your-face statement that she'd come to expect from him.

"I'm in love with you, Fay, probably have been for months, and I want more from you than toe-curling sex, sassy talk and land. I understand you might not feel the same thing or want to, but I'll do what I please."

Because his brief speech had ended on a growl and the look in his eyes was an interesting mix of soberness and macho defiance, Chase looked anything but intimidated, but Fay felt a rush of eye-stinging emotion as she remembered the words before that: *I'd sooner face a wild bull in a box than lay my heart at the feet of Fay Sheridan Rafferty.*

Chase's dark brows came together in concern and suddenly he was hunkered down in front of her chair with her hands trapped in the hard, callused warmth of his. "Well, hell, baby—are those tears?"

Fay giggled a little and gripped his hands. "Yes, they are, and yes, I meant what I said the other night. It took me a few days to get over the shock, but it's true. I love you."

She grabbed for his neck and pulled him close to kiss him. Chase was more than ready for her onslaught and swept her up to kiss her back until they were both breathless. Then he broke off the kiss to carry her to the bed, bracing a knee on the mattress as he followed her down. The rattle and thump of the drugstore bag hitting the floor reminded Fay she'd tossed it and her handbag onto the foot of the bed when she'd gotten home.

Chase mumbled something that sounded like, "Hell with that," as he started to kiss her again, but Fay slipped her fingers between their mouths to stop him. He pulled back a little, but he didn't look pleased. "It wasn't anything breakable, was it?"

"Did you really mean it, Chase?"

His dark brows came together in impatient swirls. "Mean what? That I'm in love with you?" He answered right away. "I'm in love with you." A glint of perception showed in his eyes. "And you're going to have to put up with me until we're both too crippled to sit on anything but a pair of rocking chairs out on the patio."

Another rush of tears dampened her lashes as she moved her hand to his strong jaw. "Then you might want to know what's in the bag we knocked off the bed."

Chase gave a good-natured growl and levered himself away from her to retrieve her handbag, which he set on the night table, and the drugstore sack. Fay sat up and slid to the head of the bed to watch as he opened the bag. He pulled out the huge bottle of vitamins, scanned the label, then set them next to her handbag. He finally pulled the thick hardcover book out of the sack and turned it to read the front cover.

"Everything—" He cut himself off as he read the long title. After a few moments of staring at it, taking it in, his gaze slowly came up and arrowed straight into hers. "Is this your book...or did you buy it for someone else?"

"It's mine, though you might want to read it for yourself." Fay smiled as she added, "Daddy."

A slow grin spread over Chase's handsome mouth. "When?"

"Just under seven months to go."

"It was our wedding night, wasn't it?"

"That'd be my guess. Or that morning on the creek bank."

Chase stared down at the book cover again, still a little in shock. Or maybe more than a little since he'd apparently forgotten how hot and involved they'd just been. He tossed the sack to the night table and got into bed beside her, wrapping his arm around her shoulders before he opened the book.

He'd been trying to open it across both her lap and his, and as he tried to position it, the book opened to a photo of twins that they both looked at.

"Think we'll get at least one set of those?" he asked and looked at her. Fay smiled.

"I hope so." Then she reached up and drew his head down for a long, sultry kiss that soon made Chase set the book on the night table, knocking off the vitamin bottle and her handbag before they scooted down on the bed and tenderly took up where they'd left off.

Enjoy the drama, explore the emotions, experience the relationships

4 brand-new titles each month

Available on the third Friday of every month
from WHSmith, ASDA, Tesco
and all good bookshops
www.millsandboon.co.uk

GEN/38/RTL11

0907/02

MILLS & BOON
Romance

On sale 5th October 2007

From elegant France to stylish Italy and the rugged Australian mountains – whether she's having the boss's baby, or being rescued by a millionaire, let Mills & Boon® Romance take you from laughter to tears and back again!

THE MEDITERRANEAN REBEL'S BRIDE *by Lucy Gordon*

Join Polly as she gives Italian playboy Ruggiero the surprise news that he's become a father. Another one of the ***Rinucci Brothers*** meets his match!

FOUND: HER LONG-LOST HUSBAND *by Jackie Braun*

Claire's never forgotten her short-lived marriage to Ethan. She sets out to find him and change their lives for ever... The last of the magnificent ***Secrets We Keep*** trilogy.

THE DUKE'S BABY *by Rebecca Winters*

All French *duc* Lance wants is to hold a child in his arms and be called "Daddy" and then he meets Andrea who is pregnant, widowed and melts his hardened heart...

MILLIONAIRE TO THE RESCUE *by Ally Blake*

Knight-in-shining-armour Daniel sweeps broken-hearted Brooke away to his luxurious mountain estate...for one happily-ever-after you won't want to miss.

Available at WHSmith, Tesco, ASDA, and all good bookshops
www.millsandboon.co.uk

1107/02/MB108

New York Times bestselling author

DIANA PALMER

is coming to

MILLS & BOON® *Romance*

Pure romance, pure emotion

Curl up and relax with her brand new *Long, Tall Texans* story

Winter Roses

Watch the sparks fly in this vibrant, compelling romance as gorgeous, irresistible rancher Stuart York meets his match in innocent but feisty Ivy Conley…

"Nobody tops Diana Palmer when it comes to delivering pure, undiluted romance. I love her stories."
—*New York Times* bestselling author Jayne Ann Krentz

On sale 2nd November 2007

Available at WHSmith, Tesco, ASDA, and all good bookshops

www.millsandboon.co.uk

0907/05a

On sale
5th October 2007

In October 2007
Mills & Boon present two classic collections,
each featuring three gorgeous romances
by three of our bestselling authors...

Mistress Material

Featuring

The Billionaire's Pregnant Mistress by Lucy Monroe
The Married Mistress by Kate Walker
His Trophy Mistress by Daphne Clair

Available at WHSmith, Tesco, ASDA, and all good bookshops
www.millsandboon.co.uk

0907/05b

On sale
5th October 2007

Don't miss out on these superb stories!

Wedding Bells

Featuring

Contract Bride by Susan Fox
The Last-Minute Marriage by Marion Lennox
The Bride Assignment by Leigh Michaels

Available at WHSmith, Tesco, ASDA, and all good bookshops
www.millsandboon.co.uk

4 Books
and a surprise gift!

We would like to take this opportunity to thank you for reading this Mills & Boon® book by offering you the chance to take FOUR more specially selected titles from the Romance series absolutely FREE! We're also making this offer to introduce you to the benefits of the Mills & Boon® Reader Service™—

- ★ **FREE home delivery**
- ★ **FREE gifts and competitions**
- ★ **FREE monthly Newsletter**
- ★ **Exclusive Reader Service offers**
- ★ **Books available before they're in the shops**

Accepting these FREE books and gift places you under no obligation to buy, you may cancel at any time, even after receiving your free shipment. Simply complete your details below and return the entire page to the address below. You don't even need a stamp!

YES! Please send me 4 free Romance books and a surprise gift. I understand that unless you hear from me, I will receive 6 superb new titles every month for just £2.89 each, postage and packing free. I am under no obligation to purchase any books and may cancel my subscription at any time. The free books and gift will be mine to keep in any case.

N7ZEF

Ms/Mrs/Miss/Mr ....Initials ....

BLOCK CAPITALS PLEASE

Surname ....

Address ....

....

....Postcode ....

Send this whole page to:
UK: FREEPOST CN81, Croydon, CR9 3WZ

Offer valid in UK only and is not available to current Mills & Boon® Reader Service™ subscribers to this series. Overseas and Eire please write for details.. We reserve the right to refuse an application and applicants must be aged 18 years or over. Only one application per household. Terms and prices subject to change without notice. Offer expires 30th November 2007. As a result of this application, you may receive offers from Harlequin Mills & Boon and other carefully selected companies. If you would prefer not to share in this opportunity please write to The Data Manager, PO Box 676, Richmond, TW9 1WU.

Mills & Boon® is a registered trademark owned by Harlequin Mills & Boon Limited.
The Mills & Boon® Reader Service™ is being used as a trademark.